BEST
WOMEN'S
EROTICA
2008

BEST
WOMEN'S
EROTICA
2008

Edited by

VIOLET BLUE

CLEIS
PRESS

Published in the United States by Cleis Press Inc.,
P.O. Box 14697, San Francisco, California 94114.

Printed in Canada.
Cover design: Scott Idleman
Cover photograph: Hans Neleman/Getty Images
Text design: Frank Wiedemann
Cleis Press logo art: Juana Alicia
First Edition.
10 9 8 7 6 5 4 3 2 1

ISBN 13: 978-1-57344-299-2

"The Lonely Onanista," by EllaRegina, © 2005 EllaRegina, was published on Literotica.com, January 28, 2007. "Lonely Onanista Living in National Monument Seeks Assistance—w4m" was posted anonymously by the author as a Craigslist.org Casual Encounters personal ad on December 22, 2005, December 26, 2005 and January 4, 2006; the latter is in the Best of Craigslist archive: http://www.craigslist.org/about/best/nyc/122599648.html.

For Jonathan

CONTENTS

INTRODUCTION: FOR ALL THE JOHNNYS

Book introductions bore me. So rather than tell you what it was like reading through hundreds of submissions to select the best—the white-knuckle ride, choicest pieces of erotica—I'll tell you something else. I'll tell you what I did amidst the madness, the longing, the fucking and the pure pleasure in all the words within these pages. I'll tell you what they made me do, and that will be your introduction to what you'll find here.

I keep pretending nothing hurts, but it does. I looked at myself in the blog mirror from last year, the archives reflecting what I was doing a year ago while working on this book's predecessor, and wished I could drown myself. I have lost so much. I have gained seven large scars I haven't told you about. They don't look so bad buried in the maze of my ink.

One Saturday in July, while I was in the thick of editing *Best Women's Erotica 2007*, Hacker Boy and I went on a wander. He is my breath. When the pain was bad, he took the miles and miles of violet blue rope I have in a box and tied me up tight, like a gift-wrapped neat little Shibari bruise. Naked, immobile, I waited for him to hurt me. He slowly, gently covered me in kisses from head to toe and back again. Nuzzled against my bonds. Held me restrained in his arms. I could not escape, and so was held down and loved. He always tells me he loves me. He fucks me, and his cock is more profound in its steel-hard sweetness than the violence of my street-hard heart.

After a North Beach wander, I wrote my weekly *San Francisco Chronicle* / SFGate column about where we went on Saturday and what we did. This is the rest of the story.

When we walked into the hungry i it was the last stop, not even an intentional visit. We felt like our expectations for "man's ruin" were giddily met with the smelly fog machine, and laughed at the eight-dollar beers—we'll take two, thanks. Not surprisingly, I was the only woman in the room not "on the clock"; the rest of the torn and trashed red seats and chairs around the stage were pockmarked with men.

We sat directly opposite the stage and took in the two brass poles, the mirrored background...and then it hit us. The loud, pulsing music was the song "Dark Entries." Onstage was a girl: pale, tattooed calves, biceps and chest. Small breasts pinned under a tight tube top. A neat faux-mohawk capped her off. She could easily have been a Fatal Beauty, or more. Hacker Boy and I gleefully nearly fought over who would tip her. He won, and she danced over to him with a huge smile and provided a panty-strap for him to deposit the fiver in, while he complimented her choice in music.

Next up was another astonishingly pale, tattooed beauty, with handfuls of natural breasts, a Louise Brooks hairstyle with a red flower pinned in it. We hadn't known we were out for blood that night, but then—it seemed—we were.

This was a first for us, individually and together. When we fuck, we tear each other's skin off; cannibalizing him in salt and sweat and semen (and sometimes blood) is a violent ballet of tenderness and going home. We feed on each other. We feed each other. Tonight, we would taste something new. I looked at the stripper with the mohawk with her angel eyes sitting by herself at the bar, and motioned her over.

The music blared and I was flying high on a day of cheap alcohol, the slamming assault of sound and lights and criminal lust. Her name was Johnny. I spoke, and leveled my gaze on both of them: "Three dances. The first one, you do him and I watch. Like I'm not even there. The next one, you dance for me, like it's just us. The last dance is both of us." Grinning, she agreed to my terms and said, "This is great. Usually guys make their girlfriends do it and they hate it. Not this time."

We all went to a couch in the side hall, where the patrons could watch if they wanted to. And they did. To my right, Johnny and Hacker Boy, looking like the sexiest writhing sandwich ever. She curled and arched over him, straddled and ground slowly. He focused on her and only her, and I observed what this is like—this heat and intensity, from him, and him only. *Is mine.* I pulled my stripy, combat-booted legs up and watched her muscles work against the black backdrop of his Ben Davises and T-shirt, his eyes closed in surrender under every inch of her tats and skin (and smiles) as she palpated and pressed in the dark and shadows. Serpentine. Like cruelty. Very good.

There was no hesitation when it was my turn, and she sunk into me like opiate into bloodstream, though whose spike was an open question. Hands pulled my hips and pressed the small of my back forward until the heat of my cunt met hers, and she smelled like vanilla and girl and hallucinations. I didn't know if I wanted to fuck her or eat her. That she might want to consume me too made me wish she would lie to me, for at least another twenty bucks. Johnny tracked my shoulders, my breasts, my stomach, my hips with skin so soft it felt like one long, burning fuck every time she lingered and pressed. I didn't need to taste her; her residue was all over my skin and tattooed there in transparent scratches and smells. I haven't been touched by a girl in a very long time. Johnny mainlined my dread and desire in the mirror of her cunt, and didn't bother to climb off me when the third song started.

Long limbed and hot, she tore at both of us and we were, for a moment, all perfect and wrecked in all the right ways; scars and tattoos, money for pleasure and draining her for a song; the mechanism of our desire. She was an altchick of sinuous perfection, sitting on Hacker Boy and holding my head to her neck. She locked her gazellelike legs around me and rose up high, taking us in, before straddling us both. All the ridiculous gender theatrics were gone, if they had ever been there, and I did not long to touch her. I longed to pay her to do more of what I said, because she did it so very well.

To ask for more would have been a miscalculation.

We careened out into the shriek and violence of North Beach at night, sidestepping around the sidewalks filled with the ugly genetic pastiche of American male posturing, saluted the Pyramid, and hailed home. Coming down my hall, a minute behind my Hacker Boy, I could only follow the trail of black clothing, deliberately placed, that led to my bed.

The next day, we walked around San Francisco, again, and laughed and wondered, *Johnny, are you queer?*

I never saw Johnny again, but wish I could read this entire book to her. That's not all I want from her, but I want no more than what she'd accept money for. I want her to lie to me. I want to walk into that torn-up, red-rimmed rummy of a piss-stained North Beach titty bar and put down a twenty and tell her to tell me she loves me. Another twenty if she tells me she's mine. And then I want to give her everything and drive into the catlike squall of her thighs and scream fingernails into her tattooed skin and let her drape her vanilla-cookie smelling flesh all over me again so I can pretend for a song that I don't have the word HATE tattooed under my tongue.

Best Women's Erotica 2008 was described by my publisher as "wicked" and the word "love" was used liberally to describe my selections—pieces of erotica from some of the hottest women authors going, brand-new writers and seasoned pros alike. Wander around, and see what you think.

Start your journey with Jacqueline Applebee's superb, "Penalty Fare," a red-hot ride along with a woman who engineers a very intense oral fantasy into getting out of misdeeds on the Underground. "Getting Sorted," by Morticia Catherine, is another London tale, in which a rain-soaked job seeker finds herself shopping for sex on phone booth adverts, only to wind up with—or in—a whole new position at the end of the very explicit, femme-domme tale. A. D. R. Forte's "Mercy" shows very little in the telling, charting the plot of a pair of white-collar coworkers whose idea of rewarding new hires involves the most exquisite power-play scenarios, including female submission and male anal penetration.

Jordana Winters is in top form with the eloquent, heated story "Peekaboo," in which a plain Jane visits a sex club to indulge in a little voyeurism, only to play a watchful part in a down-and-dirty bathroom encounter. Lyrical, moody and sweet with lovemaking and longing is R. Gay's "Strangers in the Water," a literal trip back in time for a woman seeking her roots in Haiti only to become drawn into recreating a moment of sexual power—and release—pivotal to her family's and country's history. Lola David's "Unicorn Sighting" promises a glimpse of a sexual animal just as rare but no less desired; here, a couple visit a filthy adult-movie theater and wind up in the alley, creating a fantasy and image I found absolutely unforgettable.

"All the Floodgates Ever Made," if there were such a possibility, wouldn't be able to hold back the deliciousness of the spontaneous butch-femme fuck that happens in Miel Rose's playful, explicit tale. At a more serious turn, Kell Brannon's "Vienna" takes us to that glorious city of Klimt and Deco, and drops us into a couple's hard-edged sex game involving female submission and sex with a male stranger. Donna George Storey is at her absolute finest in "Wet," taking us all the way to Kyoto for an American woman's fantasy fuck, violating Japanese bathing taboos and allowing her to sink deeply into her own (with the help of a hot, dominant Japanese man).

Xan West's "Please" is a sublimely rough pool hall tale that pushes boundaries and mixes (much-desired) tear-streaked oral submission with public sex, with what could only be described as a romantic S/M finish. If that feels a bit too chilly, step out into the streets with the female protagonist in Saskia

Walker's truly excellent "Winter Heat," in which a girl finds a very yummy way to stay warm with a cute male stranger while waiting for the bus on an icy London street. The old adage goes "You Can Do Mine," and Cerise Noire's tale by that name involves much more than turnabout is fair play with a girl, her boyfriend, and everyone's favorite third, a strap-on.

Amy Wadhams must know some pretty tough girls; the young woman in "Blame" ditches her family and deflowers a young man, with no regrets in a startling mix of taboos, making for one of the most edgy sexual encounters in the entire collection. Far more playful but no less edgy and intense is Jessica Lennox's "Blowjob," in which a girl gets exactly that in a lip-licking girl-girl tryst. The giddy and hot "The Bad Poet," by skilled author Kay Jaybee, mixes the hilarity of bad wordsmithing with S/M punishment, and results in a fantastic tale of male submission, female dominance and a little whipping for flavor.

In the dreamy, delirious fantasy "Flowergirl Meets Bomb," talented author msprism describes a female slave's sexual initiation at the hands of her inconceivably wealthy Mistress in a scene that seems out of time and dressed in a style reminiscent of Aubrey Beardsley's *fin de siècle* decadence. "Her(His)Story," by K. L. Gillespie, is a nearly psychedelic trip into the mind of a woman fascinated with having a penis, complete with a fantastical twist. From the pages of Craigslist comes "The Lonely Onanista" by EllaRegina, who began by creating a series of eleven Casual Encounters ads—proposing anonymous public sex with a nasty twist or two—but ended up writing a collection of incredible (and much-clicked-on) stories.

"Lost At Sea," by Peony, had to be read aloud to Hacker Boy right out of the email window with no hesitation, and equal parts lust and longing to make him mine on the spot—though the story is about the true aftermath of sucking and fucking, the deliciousness of sexual regret, and catharsis. Don't let that keep you from looking through one of the gems of this collection, Scarlett French's "Rear Window," featuring a girl whom I'd love to trade places with. Once she moves into her new place, she discovers she's got the best view in the city (though don't tell her gay neighbors). To finish your wanderings, go back to college with one of the erotic fiction masters: Alison Tyler's "Matthew, Mark, Luke and John" may be a sort of sacrilege, but it's a truly decadent one. Here, a woman finds herself trying to tutor fellow students in a Christian Iconography course, only to glean new insight on the apostles in her dorm room. Taboo in so many ways.

I hope you enjoy reading this book as much as I did putting it together. Happy wanderings.

Violet Blue
September 2007

PENALTY FARE

Jacqueline Applebee

It was supposed to be my punishment. I'm sure the train guard thought it was only right and just that I should introduce my lips to his hard-on, as penalty for traveling on the railway without a valid ticket. He had given me a simple choice; I was either to pay a week's wages as a fine, or I was to give him a blowjob the next time we met.

I guessed he didn't know how little I earn.

That's why I found myself on the 8:30 service from London Paddington to Bristol Temple Meads the next Friday morning. I waited quietly in my seat by the aisle as the train pulled out of the station in a series of long slow jerks. At first I wanted to find him, to try to keep control of the situation, but I couldn't move; I was far too nervous. As the onboard speakers crackled to life, I wondered if it was his smooth voice that I heard, welcoming everyone to the train, telling us all to observe the safety notices and that no smoking was allowed.

Ten agonizingly long minutes passed before I saw him at the other end of the narrow swaying carriage, checking tickets, collecting money and pointing the way to the buffet car in an efficient manner. Dressed as he was in his dark uniform, the crisp pressed trousers, jacket and tie made him look severe, almost intimidating. He seemed taller, more solid than before and for a split second, I was hesitant that I could really do this. Then I started thinking that he wouldn't even remember our sordid agreement; he probably wouldn't remember me. And as if he had heard my thoughts, he looked ahead and he saw me; the only black woman on the train by my estimate. I stood out from the pinstripe suits around me and amongst all the stiff uniforms of gray and white, I was like a big black target, dressed in my colorful West African outfit, chunky silver jewelry and a headwrap topping it all off. If I couldn't move before, I was frozen to the spot now.

Once our eyes met, he zeroed in on me, marching quickly through the carriage and ignoring the other passengers who held out their tickets for him to check. He slung his portable ticket machine over his shoulder as he reached my seat and he yanked me out of my chair, without even breaking his stride.

His big firm hand clamped down as a solid weight upon my shoulder and I half stumbled ahead of him. Other passengers looked at me with sympathy; they were probably thinking that I was going to be thrown bodily off the train for breaking the rules and I kept my eyes averted, not wanting to look at anyone we passed. I was directed in hurried silence to the front of the train, to the first class carriage where no one sat.

As we reached the private toilets there, I saw a sign on the door that almost made me smile. OUT OF ORDER was taped up in big red letters. I suppose that what we were about to do could be considered out of order, but I was just too horny to dwell on it.

You see, this was my choice, my dream; to be so naughty that I simply had to be punished. It had taken three trips to get into trouble and believe me when I say I had tried. But no one checked the tickets on the first journey to Oxford, the train guard on the second trip to Bath Spa took pity on me and said he'd overlook it. It was only on the third journey that I got lucky at last; this guard actually took me aside, leaned over me and told me that there was more than one way to pay for my crime. He had stared at my chest the whole time, with twinkling blue eyes lapping up the sight of me as if I were completely edible, and then he said he'd always wanted to try out a black girl.

I almost came on the spot.

Don't get me wrong; I think of myself as being reasonably smart. I know I'm not supposed to like things like this, but I do. I like them an awful lot. And just the thought of what was about to happen made me feel so damn hot! Because even though I can look as exotic as you like, I've never ever felt it.

Really, not ever.

I was born and brought up in East London, talk with a Cockney accent when I get excited and the closest I've got to the tropics is buying a tin of pineapple chunks in my local supermarket. So when my need to be bad gets tangled up with my need to feel like a sultry dusky maiden...well it's not too hard to work out why I jumped at his yummy proposal. He might have some island beauty stereotype floating around his head and tugging at his groin, but I have my stereotypes too and they make me hunger for firm pink skin, blue veins snaking around hard muscles and hair that is soft and straight. Big strong men who look like Viking warriors make me gaga with desire. Getting them to notice me is something that I've worked long and hard at.

Back on the train, I inhaled deeply as the guard reached around me. I could feel his hot breath against the back of my neck, making me shiver with anticipation. His scent caught my nose; his cologne was crisp, masculine and underlined his attributes.

He used a little funny shaped key to open the door to the restroom and then ushered me inside with a firm push. I glanced around nervously; the room was not large and neither of us was small. I looked back at him with a hint of uncertainty; he was a big handsome man and my layers of bright African cloth hid my voluptuous curves. I didn't know if we were going to fit, but he smiled at me—a lazy crooked grin that let me know that he'd done this before—and then he promptly squeezed in behind me.

As the door shut, I caught a glimpse of the bright green countryside as it blurred past the window outside; I saw the freedom of open spaces that I didn't want. I'd much rather be locked up thank you very much.

We finally made it in, although we had to dance in a tight awkward shuffle to get the door fully closed. For a moment, we both stood there in the confined space, looking at each other. Then his hands moved to his thick belt and he quickly undid the silver buckle. I took it as a cue to sink to my knees and lifted the hem of my bright yellow dress as I stooped down. The stale damp smell of the toilet was worse down at this level but I tried not to notice. I heard the slow metallic slide of his zipper and I forgot everything else as the sound hypnotized me. His dark uniform trousers dropped to the floor, pooling around thick strong-looking calves, with a mass of fine blond hairs decorating his ivory skin. He was more than ready for me and as I caught my first sight of his cock, it seemed as if there was even less space in the room than before. His large thick crimson dick radiated heat that I could already feel against my lips. It bobbed with the trundle of the train, standing in front of my face like it was a third person in the room.

I pressed my warm face to his burning cock, rubbed my cheeks, my lips over the smooth surface until I felt a hand on my head, stilling me. I heard his low voice; the first thing he'd said to me.

"Train's due at Reading station in five minutes."

I got the hint—make it quick, no fancy stuff. I could do that.

I looked back up at his cock and opened wide. I conjured up the taste of salt and placed my lips against a bead of his juice leaking from the tip. He shivered against me and I smiled as I descended on him further. I sucked steadily and slowly on his length and he gasped, almost stepping away from the intensity.

The weight of his hefty cock made my tongue bend beneath it. He felt immense inside me but I wanted it all. I licked the head with short urgent laps and the train began to shudder with me, keeping pace with my tongue. I closed my eyes, breathed out and swallowed him deeper in slow wet gulps just as we entered a tunnel. The only reason I knew this, was because my ears popped and when I swallowed again from instinct to relieve the pressure, he made a strangled noise. I felt his strong wide hands fisting the fabric of my headscarf and he pulled me forward even more.

My gag reflex is something that I have learned to live with; I've practiced on bananas and jumbo hotdogs, pushing them against the back of my throat, half swallowing them and then pulling out before I choked. So when I relaxed my jaw muscles and drew every last inch of him into me, I was as prepared as I could be. I sensed his surprise at this and he surged inside, growing impossibly harder against the roof of my mouth, stretching me to the limit.

I cupped his heavy hot balls and he went up on tiptoes, straining in the swaying room. Both of his hands were now buried in the cloth that covered my head and they were no longer guiding me, but rather he was using me to steady himself. I was half glad that he lost control so quickly, half proud of my abilities.

My slow in-and-out motions made him grunt like a bull, my nibbles made him pant like a horse and quick twists of my swollen lips made him gurgle low in his throat. He was making so many appreciative noises and seemed to be enjoying the experience so much that it was only when we felt the pull of the brakes that he suddenly stiffened against me, swore out loud and practically popped himself out of my hungry mouth.

I was amazed at the speed with which he moved; he was tucked in and dressed almost before I could pull off the blueberry condom that I had sneaked on with my first kiss to his cock.

He disappeared out the door and within moments I could hear his breathless voice announcing the next station, warning passengers to please mind the gap between the train and the platform and reminding them that we were due in Bristol at ten o'clock.

Even though the train was stationary, I still felt the strange swoon wash over me; the feeling that I was still moving, still roaring through the countryside on this pleasure train. I felt my knees start to ache, but I wasn't about to move from my position. I wrapped the purple condom in a tissue and fished just under the edge of my headwrap for a strawberry flavored one instead. That just left the mint and vanilla ones scratching at my scalp, reminding me of the possibilities.

The jerk of the train as it got going once more sent a sudden welcoming jolt to my clit. The strong series of motions as the locomotive gathered speed threatened to pull my orgasm from me, from my overexcited body and right down to the thundering wheels below.

Within seconds he came back into the room, looking at me with surprise, as if he'd thought I wasn't going to be here when he returned, but I wasn't done with him yet.

"Drop 'em," I said cheekily and he laughed and lowered his trousers once more.

This time I was fully relaxed and eager to have him in my mouth again. My previous actions had made me even more of a slut than before and I was very pleased at my progress. I was determined to suck this man dry, to have my fun.

He seemed more desperately horny than earlier and after a few enthusiastic kisses, his cock grew back to its rock-hard status, gliding into my mouth smoothly and deeply.

The guard became more vocal as he reached his peak, grunting out garbled words and curses as he thrust into me, using my mouth for his sweet sordid pleasure. I was torn between reaching up to pull him down by his dangling tie and staying where I was, to get off on the rumbling between my legs. I thought briefly about how my brain got addled when I was horny but it was worth it, as being bad felt so much better than I could have ever imagined. Every part of me tingled and vibrated with the train and I gripped the base of his cock and felt him almost topple over.

My decision was made and I lowered myself down further until my pussy was directly atop the shaking floor. I came quickly with a muffled shout around the cock in my mouth, the orgasm rattling my body with a pounding, roaring sensation that thundered through my bones, like the speeding train I rode in.

The guard's ticket machine was still strapped to his back and it made a noise as loud as both of our cries as he jerked against the door, his jagged movements accidentally pressing the buttons on the device while he rocked into me. I sucked hard, drawing out his come in full strong motions and he groaned long and loud, flicking his hips in sharp shudders. I felt the condom swell within my mouth, tasted strawberry milkshake and withdrew after a sweet blissful moment.

I banged the back of my head against the washbasin as I clambered up stiffly; my knees were killing me and I was damp in places even I was surprised at. He sighed out loud and looked completely spent, but was quick enough to see me put the second condom in some tissue. He reached down and gripped the head of his cock, swiped a drop of come that had leaked out and held it up to me as if to dare me to lick it from his thick fingers, but I had other plans. I wanted a mark from this event, apart from the bruise to the back of my head. I wanted a reminder that it hadn't all been my sex-crazed imagination, so I offered my hands to him and he knew what to do; he smeared a white dribble of his come across my wrists, dabbed a drop behind each ear and stroked the last of it into the cleavage of my breasts. We both smiled in a conspiratorial way as he adorned me; we both knew that I would wear him like perfume all day, would carry a part of him back home to the East End of London.

"That was cracking," he exclaimed in a lazy satisfied voice. "God I could get into so much trouble for this, could get myself fired..." he paused and then winked at me, smiling broadly. "But you're worth it sweetheart!"

He turned to the door and was about to leave when suddenly a long beep rang out. A concertina strand of tickets ejected themselves from his machine; four singles going all the way to the end of the line.

Maybe we'll do that next time.

GETTING SORTED

Morticia Catherine

The rain begins to pour down in torrents. It's one of those summer afternoons when the sky begins to darken and then just opens.

As usual I am totally unprepared for the change in weather, dressed only in a summer dress and open sandals. I seek shelter in the nearest telephone box, but in the few seconds it takes me to struggle with the door, I am soaked to the skin.

Shivering inside amid the smell of stale fags and urine, I weigh up my options. I'll most certainly wait for the rain to stop, but what then? I don't want to go home really, it has been such a long journey up here and I don't want to waste the rest of the day. After all Paul insisted that I get myself sorted out.

Glancing down at myself I realize that the

light summer dress is probably showing more of me than I want. My nipples are standing out like small doorknobs. They are so hard from the cold they began to hurt. I casually pass my hand over my chest and feel them against my palm. It feels good and I have to stop myself from doing it again.

I glance around the box: everywhere are cards, stickers and notices for various sexual services. I casually wonder how you could choose between "Busty Blonde" or "Horny, Wet and Willing". I look outside, but it is still raining hard and the pavement's awash. I look back at the notices. There is a picture of 44DD with a pouting cherry mouth cupping her large tits. Jostling for space above the emergency numbers is "Miss Correction" who promises to spank you till you come.

By the time I have read a lurid notice for "Suck My Dripping Pussy", I am a bit unnerved to find my nipples are standing out from more than the cold. I wonder if many women ring these services. Now, I'm not a lesbian, yet nothing turns me on as much as the promise of some girl-on-girl action. I begin to scan the notices again. If I was to ring one I would have to be sure they did girls. I start looking again: "Ready, Wet and Waiting" has me feeling a distinct flick from my clit, which is getting harder by the minute.

What am I doing? I couldn't possibly be considering this, could I? But I have time on my hands, no one is expecting me back till later and Paul was quite emphatic about my sorting myself out.

I think about Paul, and wonder if he would be shocked at what I'm considering. I am still pondering this when I spot a card sticking out of the actual metal phone holder. It reads "Sexy Bi Redhead, Big Tits, Hard Tongue." I pull the card out. Now that would be perfect.

My heart is beating fast and I feel that racing in my veins you get from daring to do something you shouldn't.

I know it's now or never and as I rummage in my bag for phone change I tell myself I could always not turn up. I find a pound coin in the bottom recesses of my bag, covered in, well I'm not sure what really, handbag stuff.

I put the coin in and dial the number. I expect it to ring and ring, or be engaged, or go into voicemail, but within two rings a voice says, "Hello." My voice dries up in my throat. "Hello," she repeats.

"Hello" I croak. "I've got your number, from—err—a card." I pause. "In a phone booth."

"Oh yes," she says. "Do you want to book an appointment?"

"Yes," I stammer.

"When would you like to come?" she purrs.

"Now. I would like to come now..." and then I add, "if that's possible." In fact I feel like I am going to come right there in the phone booth. My clit feels so full of pressure that my pussy lips hurt.

There is a pause before she answers. "Okay, I'm free this afternoon."

"That's great," I croak. I fumble in my bag to find a pen to write down the address, which is somewhere in Hampstead that I don't know. This isn't really surprising, as I have only ever driven through Hampstead once. "I'll see you in about 20 minutes," I rasp. I put the phone down and leave the phone booth. Pushing any doubts I have behind a wall in my mind, I hail a taxi.

As the warmth from the rear heaters brushes my legs I begin to feel warm and relaxed, and most definitely turned on. The muscles in my legs feel tingly. I keep squeezing my buttocks together, enjoying the sensation of my pussy tightening.

I am jolted out of my little sexual bubble by being catapulted off the seat as the taxi pulls to a stop outside a Victorian terrace. "Here you are, Miss, that'll be five pounds eighty." The cabdriver couldn't give a toss what I'm doing here, but I am still convinced he knows. I hand him seven pounds and flee.

The cab has left me right outside number five. I had convinced myself it would be a seedy bedsit, but number five seems to be a whole house. I take a deep breath, walk up the path and ring the bell.

A smartly dressed woman in her late fifties, with neat bobbed gray hair, answers the door. I knew it was too good to be true, the card was a ploy to sell me Amway. She smiles at me and says, "You must be the three o'clock." As she shows me into a small sitting room I wonder if I have accidentally booked a dental appointment. That is until I see the magazines on the table. A range of high-quality porn is spread invitingly across the polished wooden surface.

I am startled by the sound of a gentle cough. The smartly dressed woman is standing in the doorway. She smiles and says, "My mistress will see you now. Shall I take your bag?" I dumbly hand it to her. She pauses as she takes it. "This is your first time, isn't it? Don't be embarrassed. We are very discreet. This way." I am obviously not expected to reply.

I follow her along the cream-colored hall, our feet making no sound on the thick carpet. I briefly think of my own carpet, and how thin it is. She stops in front of a heavy oak door with an ornate handle. She knocks and enters, leaving me standing outside like an errant servant. I hear her say, "Mistress, it's your three o'clock appointment," then she steps aside to let me pass.

I don't know what I had expected, but not this. The room is beautifully decorated with heavy drapes and two ornate loungers. A gilt-edged mirror that almost fills one wall hangs opposite a wooden four-poster bed hung with curtains. It feels...it feels like a place of worship, and in the middle of all of this, framed by the window, is the priestess.

She has long red hair down to the middle of her back, its natural waves framing her elegant face, with green eyes and high cheekbones. Her mouth, full and slick with red lipstick, is balanced by a delicately jutting chin. Her breasts are full and creamy, rising up and down from the confines of a corset made from red satin. Its silkiness is enhanced by a covering of black lace that cups those full breasts and frames the hips and groin of its wearer. Her thighs and legs are encased in black stockings. The delicious six-inch creamy gap between stocking top and knickers is tantalizing. She's also wearing pointed lace-up boots to midcalf. All of this, glimpsed between swirls of her satin dressing gown.

When at last she speaks her voice is like silk, tinged with something distantly European. "Please sit." She gestures to the chaise lounge. "Would you like a drink? Some wine?"

"Thank you," I reply. She pours a glass from bottle already open on a silver tray. As she hands it to me, I notice her fingers, long and slim, tipped with crimson.

I sip the wine, and welcome the quick warm buzz it gives me. "This is your first time isn't it?" I look up startled. "It's okay." She smiles, and goes on before I have time to answer. "I can tell by the way you look. I don't see many women, as clients," she laughs. "You will be a welcome diversion from a day full of cocks."

"Thanks, I think," I stammer, sipping the wine again. "You have a beautiful home."

"Thank you," she replies. "Now, you didn't come here to talk about my interior decoration. Time is pressing—what would you like?"

"I don't know, I'm...I'm..." I pause, suddenly overwhelmed. She takes the glass from my hand.

"Why don't you leave it to me, and we can take it from there." And with that, while I watch her from where I am sitting on the chaise lounge, she slips the gown from her shoulders. She runs her fingers down the laces on her corset, then gently pulls me to my feet. She turns me around, and pushes herself against my back, rubbing her hands over my body, feeling my breasts through the dress. Gently she turns me to face her and eases me onto the sofa, straddling my legs as I sit down. I put my hands on her creamy thighs while she undoes the buttons on my dress. I can feel the heat from her crotch on my belly. I reach up and touch the rise of her breasts, wanting to see the nipples. I pull at the laces of the corset, freeing the breasts enough for them to poke out of the top. Her nipples are large and dark. They harden as I touch them. I feel out of control and think I should stop this before it goes too far, but I know it's already too late.

Her nipples harden fully as I roll my tongue around them. I push them together, putting both into my mouth. I suck them, feeling each one with my tongue and she groans and pushes me back. She reaches then to expose my own little titties, with my nipples that are almost the size of my tits. I feel them hardening and I want her to suck them, to lick them with her soft tongue like they're two hard cocks. She plunges forward, her hair spilling over my stomach as she takes them into her crimson mouth. I watch the lipstick smear over my nipples and "God, that's so horny," I manage to say, as she sucks and tugs them rigid. I gasp as she pulls them out of her mouth and moves down my stomach, kissing my flesh as she continues downward. She reaches my pussy and pushes my legs apart. Vaguely, I think how glad I am that I'm wearing my French knickers, as she runs her tongue over the fabric encasing my mound.

"You like girls," she mutters. "You bad bad girl, look at how wet you are." She licks the silk, which instantly sticks to my flesh and outlines my pussy; I ache for her to move under the fabric, but the sensation on my skin is wonderful. Her tongue flicks under the edge of the knickers; I feel the hardness of her tongue as she finds the lips of my hole. I gasp and arch my back, wanting to feel her tongue inside me. Smiling, she replaces her tongue with an index finger. She strokes and teases the edge between flesh and fabric, smiling as I grind my pelvis toward her, straining to push her inside.

At last she slips her finger in, stroking from top to bottom. "Is this what you want, you dirty bitch?" I am momentarily shocked at the words, but feel myself moisten at the same time. She brushes over my clitoris, groaning loudly, telling me how beautiful my shaved cunt looks. I push my cunt toward her digits; I want to feel the length of her fingers. She's pulling them from the edge of my cunt and raising them to her lips, rubbing my juice on her crimson mouth. Taking the spit from her mouth she plunges her fingers forcefully up into my pussy. I gasp loudly as I feel them deep inside. I have a passing thought about Paul—wondering what he's doing, if he managed to find the dinner I left—but as soon as it's formed the thought is gone. The sudden removal of her fingers leaves me feeling empty, but before I have time to voice my loss she is leading me to the bed. Pushing me onto my back, she climbs up and kneels across my face.

My face is level with her mound, those stocking clad thighs within inches of my face, lickable. I grip her arse and pull her pussy toward my face, sucking and licking the fabric of her beautifully embroidered underwear. She's drenched, and I feel the nub of her clit through the fabric, slick with pussy juice; I rub the tip of my finger round it in little circles.

I'm delighted to see her reach up and cup her breasts, pinching her nipples as I stroke her. I part the fabric and, with my fingers deep inside her, I ease her up until we are both on our knees facing each other. I ease another finger in and she groans and tilts her head back: "More, fuck me harder," she spits. Getting the message, I don't bother to be gentle; I have lost all pretense of shyness as my pleasure grows. She is so wet it's easy to fit four fingers inside her, using my thumb to rub her clit. I wonder what's the biggest cock she's ever had, and thinking about her servicing one makes a wave of wetness flow down onto my thigh. I pump furiously, catching my other hand in her long red hair as she grinds down. Suddenly she grabs at my wrist, making me stop. I lie down on the bed, knowing that if she puts her leg between mine I will come; she knows that too, and she ties me spread-eagle to the bed, using the silk restraints that are already there.

I've slept with girls before, drunken fumblings with mates who didn't lick pussy but certainly didn't mind if you did, leaving me unsatisfied and wanting more. This is the real thing, though, and my heart is hammering as she kneels between my legs and latches onto my clit. Using the wetness from my pussy she soaks her finger and pushes against my arse. I struggle against my ties, crying "No," but she rakes one fingernail against my clit, bends down and latches on with that crimson mouth to soothe it, and pushes her finger into my arsehole. I can feel my orgasm building. She pauses, removes her finger and unties my legs and positions herself between them until her clit and wet lips are kissing against mine.

Then she begins to move her pussy gently against mine and I groan helplessly. My own moans are matched by hers and I watch as her beautiful snatch with its smear of auburn hair grinds down to rub against me. As I begin to climax she increases her pace, rubbing her clit mercilessly into mine as she too begins to come.

As we lie panting on the bed, she asks, "Was that everything you had hoped for?"

"Oh yes," I answer, laughing. There is a sharp rap on the door.

"Mistress, your five o'clock is here."

"Thank you Jean, I'll be fifteen minutes."

I sit up too. I suddenly feel awkward. "Look, I'd better go... Thanks... Do I see Jean on the way out?"

She doesn't say anything for what seems like forever, then turns to face me. "Look, I know this isn't very usual."

I laugh. "None of this is usual."

She smiles and sits down. "Look, I really need a favor. If I waiver the charge, will you help me out this evening? See, the client coming in next pays really well. He wanted two girls and I was meant to sort it out, only I saw you instead and it sort of slipped my mind."

I can't believe what I'm hearing. "Are you serious?"

"Yes," she says. I know from her face that she is. "You wouldn't have to fuck him, I'd do that." An image flashes into my mind that makes my pussy twitch.

"Just be my slave, let me touch you in front of him, that sort of stuff." She bites her bottom lip. "Look, think about it while I change." And with that she bounces off the bed and heads toward an adjoining door.

I get up and follow her to the door. My brain is doing overtime. "Okay, this is all a bit crazy, but okay...on one condition." She pauses from fastening some wicked looking straps.

"What's that?"

I laugh again. "Will you tell me your name?"

"Ketha," she replies without looking up.

"I'm Kate," I say, smiling. She laughs now and suddenly this all doesn't seem quite so crazy.

She does up the PVC catsuit covered in straps and zips. It's zipped under the crotch and over the breasts. Her feet are now encased in boots with the thinnest stiletto heels I have ever seen. She looks like PVC sex goddess. She hands me a leather swimsuit, split to the navel. I start to put it on, not an easy task, and Ketha has to help me out as I work my way into it back to front. She slips a dog collar around my neck and fastens it just as there's a knock on the door. I suddenly feel self-conscious.

"Enter" she calls. Jean enters, looks slightly bemused, and says, "Your five o'clock, Mistress."

Ketha smiles. "Thank you, Jean. Send him in." Ketha hardly has time to whisper, "Just do as I say," before a middle-aged man steps into the room. He is slightly graying, but lean, in a banker's suit. He looks approvingly at the pair of us.

He undresses and lies on the bed. My pussy starts to moisten and I know then that I won't be just watching. The banker's cock twitches and grows as he watches Ketha hold my chain tight and direct me to taste her cunt, which I do thoroughly as any good servant would. As I lick her out, Ketha's crimson mouth is filled with his swollen cock. When I feel her gently yank my chain I just know I have to position myself over his face. Still working on Ketha's hole, I lift my leg over his face until my pussy is level with his mouth, and he reaches up and undoes my zipper. My pussy swells out of the hole and I grind my split crotch onto his mouth. I feel the cold edges of the zipper against the fullness of my pulsing pussy. Ketha looks back and smiles, her mouth full of cock. The banker licks my pussy frantically, and my juices drip onto his chin. I think about him at his desk at work; think about him tending his garden; think about him later, wanking over today, and I grind my pussy down. His tongue pokes its way into my entrance and I touch my nipples as I think about him taking his plump cock in hand. Ketha removes his cock from her mouth and squats her beautiful cunt over it while she kisses me, sharing the taste of the banker's pre-come. I kiss her more and more deeply, sucking the banker's taste from her tongue.

She holds the chain tight while I bend to lick her pussy lips, which are now spread over the banker's thick shaft. As I tease the banker with my engorged pussy I catch sight of the three of us in the mirror. We look dirty and beautiful all at the same time and I love the way it frames us. As I bend down again to reach round with my tongue and pleasure her clit, we speak only in low groans, punctuated by short requests from the banker.

Now I have always found the thought of anal slightly sordid, but when Ketha bends over to allow the banker to take possession of her tight hole, I slip two fingers full of lube into her. Ketha's arse is filled with the banker's fat member, and I bend over to let her fill mine with her stiletto; she exquisitely times her thrusts with yanks on the chain. Just when I think I can't take any more she guides the banker's dick into my aching hole; while I bend over with the banker's cock stretching my pussy, my face is wet with Ketha's juices. Sucking her swollen clit seems doubly exciting to the background of the banker's grunts. He gropes at my hips as he plunges in and out of my slick cleft. Tells me he has never felt so good, that my pussy is so tight. Then Ketha uses the chain to pull me from the banker's cock.

Steering me around like a trotting pony, she guides his engorged muscle into my mouth. Behind me, the sound of buckles, followed by a firm nudging at my cunt lips. Using the juices from my hole she slicks the strap-on before pushing it into my pussy. Using the reins, she guides me back onto the thick leather strap-on and begins to ride me. I feel my juices sliding out and Ketha uses them to moisten my arse. When it's wet enough, Ketha nudges the rigid leather of the strap-on at the sensitive folds of my arse. Gently, she begins to fill my arse with the strap-on. There is no resistance, but still she is slow and persistent, waiting for my tight little arse to grab each push of the hard leather cock before she continues. I cry out as she opens me up fully; I can't believe how wonderful my arse feels, so full of leather cock. I bend and fill my mouth with the banker's swollen penis as he makes encouraging noises.

As the banker finally shoots his load, Ketha and I are licking his balls, and concentrating more on each other's tongues as we enjoy licking the thick drizzle of his sperm from each other's lips.

The banker lies back against the embroidered pillows of the bed and watches as we bring ourselves to climax with our mouths. Each of us is clamped onto the other's clit, almost forgetting about the banker's presence. As Ketha's clit swells in my mouth and the sweet, thick cream of her beautiful cunt slides down my chin, I glance sideways at him, feeling sexy and powerful as he gently strokes his cock.

After the banker leaves, Ketha and I share a shower and dress. Ketha says, "You should borrow a jumper, it's cold out now the rain's stopped."

Smiling, I say, "If I borrow a jumper I would have to return it."

She pauses. "That's okay, we make a good team, and the banker paid double." She hands me a wad of notes. I stare at them, but she puts her hand on my shoulder. "You earned it."

As the rhythm of the train lulls me into semiconsciousness, I'm vaguely aware of passing from one world into another.

Paul is standing on the platform as the train pulls in. "Nice jumper. How did the job hunting go, did you get anything sorted?"

"As it happens I think I've found just the right job."

"That's great, just don't go bringing the work home with you," he teases.

I smile at him. "Don't worry—I don't think there's any danger of that."

MERCY

A. D. R. Forte

Picture the cast of characters: Rhys—dark hair just a little too long at the neck, tie loosened slightly because it's hot here at the hotel bar, pretty-boy mouth set in that unintentional but totally fuckable pout so at odds with his seriousness; Kyle—half a head taller than every man in the room, blue eyes, wearing the power suit to end all power suits; charisma and control in different ways.

And me staring at both of them over my glass of cabernet, my mind so deep in the gutter I'm afraid I'll need scuba gear to find it and drag it out again. Although with men like these to look at, why would I want it out of the gutter?

Tonight at least Rhys is smiling, glowing with success over his promotion. Between the three of us, we've polished off one bottle of cabernet already and we're almost through with the second. Kyle is telling us a story from a past life—this one about catching a couple of employees in the act, and how we ended up on the topic I'll never know, but I love it. Rhys's face is red; he's trying not to glance my way as Kyle foreshadows the denouement; failing because I'm sitting right at his elbow and he has to be able to feel the heat of my body.

"So we finally use the manual override to unstick the dock door, get the damn thing open and I go over to the control room." Kyle pauses to take a sip of wine and chuckle before he goes on.

"And mind you, there's half the night crew and the entire morning crew standing there. So I open the door and there's this girl with her big, juicy ass—forgive me Lauren—her ass propped right on top of the dock controls and one of the techs is just bangin' the hell out of her."

Kyle pauses for dramatic effect before delivering the punch line with a wicked grin, and Rhys's face is redder than the wine stain on his napkin.

"And so while I'm standing there trying my damnedest not to laugh, one of my crew supervisors looks around my shoulder and goes 'Guess we weren't the only ones tryin' to deliver a load.' "

"Wh...what did you do?" I ask, when I can stop laughing long enough to breathe and wipe my eyes. Rhys still can't talk, but damn he's irresistible when he relaxes that adamantine composure and laughs. I want him like that; without restraint.

Kyle shrugs. "Suspended them both for a week. I figured the embarrassment was punishment enough."

"You're the very soul of understanding, Kyle."

He meets my gaze across the table and grins. "I always try to take care of my people," he says, and it's my turn to blush.

How well I know. Kyle plays the VP part so well it's enough to make you cry. He says all the right things and none of the wrong ones. When he took the job a year ago, Rhys sang his praises almost daily: Kyle was the best we'd ever worked for; he was who Rhys wanted to be in ten years. I listened and smiled, and since our fearless leader didn't raise any eyebrows, I just agreed with Rhys. Thought nothing of it.

Until a certain party the October after he started with the firm. At first, I didn't even recognize him. That could have been partly due to the leather mask, but Kyle has an unmistakable voice. Like Rhys's voice, it's deep and rich, but his inflections are lazier, Southern, educated. He can captivate listeners when he talks, whole boardrooms and conference rooms of them.

So when I overheard him talking, I almost choked on my egg roll and had to put it down and turn.

"Kyle?"

"Lauren?"

We stared at each other through our masks for a few awkward seconds. Then it hit us; we were both equally compromised by being there. Or equally matched; whichever way you want to look at it. I think we were both simply surprised at the meeting. I laughed and took his arm. He admired my dress, cut low to the waist as it was. I admired his leather trousers and boots. We danced and drank lots of wine and by the end of the night, I knew the stuff our VP was really made of. It was all hard and male and utterly, completely depraved.

He left the hotel room before I woke up, but on Monday morning there were red roses on my desk when I got to work, the card unsigned. He never said anything, and I had to respect the man for sheer class...and for other things. We never so much as hinted at it however, until the day he caught me staring at Rhys with hopeless longing on my face. Desire so naked there was no denying it. Kyle had lifted his eyebrows and I'd blushed.

"Is that what you want?" he'd asked later the same afternoon, and I nodded.

I've wanted for three years, but Rhys has old-fashioned notions of honor. We had coffee on the very first day we met; friendship was a given. He let me be his confidante, he let me into his world, but ultimately he told me no. Told me he wanted me more than he'd ever wanted anything in his life, but he didn't dare. "What if?" he said. "What if it turns into more than one night?"

I didn't have an answer.

I think he's read far too many historical novels or maybe played too much D&D. It adds to his charm, the way he strives to live by his code of lawful good no matter what, all the while looking just like a fantasy slut out of any girl's wet dream. Me, on the other hand, I just want what I want, and Rhys's recalcitrance does me no good. So when Kyle said he would think of something, I chose to believe him. Working together, Kyle and I are capable of plenty, both in the office and out of it.

"Well I don't think I've got anything to top your story," I say now, reaching for the wine bottle to refill all our glasses. "The most interesting one I can think of was the time we found two guys in the exercise room shower 'working off some steam.' "

I catch Rhys's gaze and smile. "I was actually sorry to have to break that one up. It was worth watching."

He looks away quickly and takes a swallow of his cabernet.

"And what did you do?" he asks.

I shrug. "One was a team supervisor so I had to let him go."

"No mercy from Lady Lauren," Kyle teases.

I grin and lean back, and with my jacket off, my silk power-blue shirt pulls tight against my chest and the lacy bra beneath. Rhys turns to me, serious as always, but the alcohol has done its job. He looks and looks and doesn't look away. Across the table Kyle shifts, and as I meet his gaze an unspoken message passes between us. My heart starts to beat a little faster.

"No, no mercy whatsoever," I say.

When the bar closes an hour later, we grumble and whine and polish off whatever's left in bottle number three.

"I'm so not ready for bed yet," I say.

"Neither am I," adds Kyle. "We need a nightcap."

"Champagne to celebrate," I suggest, and Kyle nods.

"Perfect." He turns to the bartender and asks him to put the order through to room service. A bottle of the good stuff to his suite.

Rhys looks from one of us to the other and shakes his head. Maybe some instinct warns him.

"You guys are kidding right?"

"No we aren't. We haven't properly celebrated you tonight," I say.

Kyle agrees as he turns back to us, ignoring Rhys's token protest that it really isn't necessary.

"So...my room?" he says. "You okay with that Lauren?"

Smart-ass.

"I think I'll be fine with that."

I take Rhys's arm.

"Come on, you don't need sleep. The night is still young."

He laughs as we leave the bar. He doesn't resist.

Kyle closes the door behind the bellboy and holds up the bottle with a smile.

"Champagne. Lauren"—his gaze moves down my torso—"maybe you'd do the honors for us?"

I guess his intent and my heart starts racing again.

"Absolutely."

While he goes to work on the cork, I stand up. I start with my pants and Rhys, sitting across the room flipping through a magazine, glances up and freezes like a trapped deer. He looks at Kyle who is busy with the champagne bottle and then his gaze swings back to me in disbelief.

My shoes aren't particularly sexy, sensible work pumps with three-inch heels, but I slip them back on after I wriggle out of pants and trouser socks. I keep them on as I slide my panties down my legs and take those off one leg at a time. Rhys's lips are parted. He watches silently, holding the magazine strategically in place while I take my shirt off. Then my bra. And I see him take a deep, slow breath.

"Perfect." I turn to find Kyle looking me over with an approving smile. "Now your hair," he adds.

I pull the clips out; tousle my curls a little as they fall free.

"Messy enough for you?" I ask, looking sideways at Kyle, and he laughs.

"Actually, I'd prefer it just a little messier." His gaze goes to my crotch and I nod.

Smiling at Rhys, who hasn't moved a muscle, I sit on the edge of the coffee table, legs apart, one hand behind me for balance.

"Kyle likes me messy, Rhys." I run my hand down my stomach, between my legs. "How would you like me?"

He shakes his head slowly, side to side. Incredulous. In

denial. This can't be happening; I can't be doing this and he can't, shouldn't, mustn't look. But I see him giving up his good intentions, and I smile as I spread my legs a little wider.

My pussy lips are already wet with need as I slide two fingers between them and trail glistening moisture up over the soft, shaved flesh, up over my bare mound. My clit tingles at the touch, wanting more, and Rhys swallows. I watch his face, imagining how hard he is behind that magazine, under those microfiber slacks, and I tease my clit, rubbing it between the sheltering folds to either side so that my touch is diminished and I'm even more frustrated. So that I'm even wetter.

Kyle has stopped fiddling with the bottle entirely, watching too now as my fingers enter my soaking pussy. My muscles clench around them and I rub hard, moaning as sweet pressure fills my cunt. I lean my head back and arch my hips upward, the wet sound of my fingers moving inside me filling the room. I don't think my gorgeous boys can so much as remember how to breathe. Even Kyle's never seen me this way; this wanton and hungry for release.

I'm so hot. I'm burning up. I'm so close and I need to come, but I stop. Panting. Straining to resist the insistent throbbing between my legs, I draw my fingers up to my chest. I rub my juices all over my hard nipples and then look at Kyle, waiting.

He fumbles into action, popping the cork on the champagne and looking at me with a dirty, dirty smile as white fizz cascades down the side of the bottle. I smile and lean further back on the coffee table. Kyle beckons Rhys over and like a sleepwalker, a man in a dream, he stands and walks over to the table.

"Ever done a champagne body shot?" Kyle asks. Rhys doesn't take his eyes off me as he shakes his head. Standing above me, he shrugs his jacket off and I see a glint in his eyes that I've never seen before.

"Never," he replies. "But that's about to change."

He smiles as he takes the bottle from Kyle and leans down, and I'm mesmerized by that smile; distracted by this new, intense, lustful Rhys. I gasp when the cold liquid hits my navel and trickles down my belly, but a second later Rhys's mouth is moving hotly down my skin, sucking and licking, stopping just before his lips touch the sensitive folds of my pussy.

I whimper in frustration, but it's Kyle's turn. He lowers me to my elbows, stretching me out across the table while he pours and licks his shot from between my breasts. Licking all around my soft curves without so much as brushing against my aching nipples.

I hate them both.

"Your turn," Kyle laughs. He's unzipping his pants, and I sit up, but I feel Rhys's hands on my waist pulling me backward. "Up on your knees," he whispers against my neck. I look over my shoulder to see him on the other side of the coffee table. His tie is gone, the first three buttons of his shirt are undone, and the glint in his eyes is brighter, wilder, more arousing than ever.

I'm shivering a little as I kneel and turn to face Kyle again. He's waiting, lazily stroking his long erection and watching me. I open my lips an inch from his magnificent cock, and he pours the shot for me. My timing is near perfect; only a few drops spill to the carpet. I catch the rest in my mouth and suck it all down, suck it off his warm hardness, and he groans. Closes his eyes.

Still sucking on Kyle, I see Rhys take the bottle from him. When cold drops hit my back and run down between my asscheeks I gasp, choking on Kyle's dick as Rhys sucks all the way down my back, biting the tender flesh on the undersides of my ass, and I moan my appreciation as he spreads my cheeks. Rhys's tongue flicks back and forth over my clit, his face pressed into my cunt and ass, and I taste Kyle's pre-come, salty on my tongue. I suck greedily at him, loving his taste, but he pulls out of my mouth and I look up, confused.

He pinches my cheek and mouths the words "bad girl" as he kneels so that his head is level with my chest. Then he drapes my arms over his shoulders so that I can support myself as he and Rhys suck and fondle my soft flesh. Making me moan and whimper. Making warm wetness trickle down my legs as their fingers and tongues roll and twist my nipples, invade my pussy. As their male kisses and rough male hands cover my skin, back and arms and thighs and belly.

I feel their tongues lapping at my clit, twisting over each other in their eagerness to drive me insane and I wonder how much it turns them on. I know Kyle's tastes; but I know Rhys would never, ever admit such desire in a million years. Yet here he is, swapping spit and pussy juice with another man.

And thinking of how far he's fallen, how much we've already corrupted him, is the last straw. My pussy tightens around Rhys's finger and I grip Kyle's shoulders hard, my knees pressing painfully into the table surface as I come; sweet, messy and sticky enough for even Kyle.

Every girl should be this lucky.

Rhys is the one to scoop me up and take me to the bed. He strips naked while I finger my still-throbbing clit, and then he bends over me, his lovely mouth open and hungry to kiss me as he parts my legs, pushing my hand away and urging the head of his thick cock against my wet opening. I squirm and arch under him, wanting to fill every inch of my pussy with his hardness, squeezing him tight as he thrusts against my aroused flesh, and over his shoulder I smile at his boss. My boss. My partner in crime.

I see Kyle, naked now, putting his own condom on and I know what comes next.

Thrilled with anticipation, wanting it because it's my pleasure as much as his, I watch him slather lube across his cock and then reach out for our beautiful boy's ass. My own buttocks tighten as Rhys's whole body goes tense and he falters, almost pulling away. But I'm looking into his eyes; I won't let his gaze slip away. I run my fingers through his hair and press my hips up into his while Kyle presses his erection to his ass, and Rhys knows he's trapped.

But then he's known it all along, somewhere deep inside. He is one of us after all.

Kyle works a lube-covered finger into him and he closes his eyes, shaking his head. Willing this not to happen. I'm thrusting gently upward under him, kissing his lips, his cheeks. Comforting him with my femininity. And he protests, but he knows it's futile.

He's saying 'No' but Kyle's dick is widening his hole, easing into him. Waiting while he tenses, and then moving again as his terrified muscles relax. I can feel every thrust with our bodies joined like this—Rhys inside of me, Kyle fucking me by proxy—and my pussy responds. I'm still wet and soft and Rhys is still hard. Even though he doesn't want to be.

The tears only escape when the head of Kyle's dick slips full into him and Kyle's length follows. All the way in. He groans and his cock spasms in me, but I lick the salt from his perfect cheekbones. I tell him he's gorgeous and that I love this, as I rub the droplets of sweat and tears on my breasts into my skin. Playing with his nipples; wriggling under him; and his cock, on the verge of going limp, becomes hard again.

Driven by Kyle's rhythm, he starts to thrust into me. His own body takes over, needing more, and I see the confusion tinted with shame on his face as he fucks me. Loving the sensation of fucking me, and being fucked. Loving the soft, sensual pleasure and the brutal pain. Hating himself for it.

We kiss his shame away. Kyle runs his fingers through his hair and kisses the back of his neck. I prop myself up on my elbows to tease his lips with my own, and finally, although he's still hurting, he manages a smile.

The force of his thrusts changes. That glint in his beautiful eyes again, he presses me back into the bed and grabs my hips. Holds me in place as he takes his pleasure, and I struggle for air, the breath knocked from me by the double force of their bodies and my muscles clenching hard around his cock. I wrap my hands around his neck and Kyle leans down to suck on my fingers as he fucks both of us. As Rhys pounds into my tight pussy and has his perfect ass rammed in turn. And I've never ever known anything like this before.

I'm moaning and grinding against Rhys; so wet I can barely feel him except for the driving pressure on my clit and in my aching pussy and I don't know where my orgasms start or end. I just know I'm digging my nails into Rhys's back and my fingers hurt, and he's coming, screaming raw and tortured and in ecstasy, his face buried against my neck. Kyle's weight crushing him into me as Kyle fucks him hard, harder. Kyle's face in Rhys's hair as he comes with a desperate cry of his own, his legs tangled with mine, his chest pinning my hands to Rhys's back. Sweet, passionate chaos.

And I think *No, no mercy whatsoever.*

We don't talk about it on Monday morning—and we won't ever talk about it—that's out of the question. But there are two sets of red roses waiting on my desk, both without cards.

PEEKABOO

Jordana Winters

A plain Jane. That's all she had ever been, and—likely—all she would ever be.

As a child, she had never heard anyone tell her parents "She's such a pretty girl." She'd known only envy and jealousy as she watched her girlfriends develop breasts, hips and curves. At thirty, her figure was like that of an adolescent girl, with bony hips and breasts that barely fit the smallest bra. She rarely studied her reflection, believing her face to be too plain and nondescript. She thought her ears stuck out too much, her hair was too straight, and her glasses made her appear brainy.

Even her name was plain. Beth. Boring one-syllable Beth.

She was passed over for jobs because she lacked the confidence to make an effort. Men rarely glanced her way. Beth would never be the hot girl at the office, the gym or the bar.

Beth was plain in everything she did, with one exception. She had a very real fetish for watching. When it had started, she didn't know. What she did know was that her hunger for it was getting worse and less easily sated.

Internet porn sites did the trick for a little while, as did the expensive telescope that was always pointed out of the window of her forty-fourth-floor condo. Watching couples fuck and men jerk off was still guaranteed to moisten her panties, but she needed more. Her cunt was unsatisfied and ached for something new.

In a bold and uncharacteristic move, Beth opted to leave the security of her home and go out amongst the rest of society's perverts. She'd been watching a certain club's website for months, waiting for the right themed costume party to present itself. She dressed in a short kilt, black knee-high socks, patent leather heeled shoes, white shirt, tie and hair worn in pigtails. She felt ridiculous, but even so it would allow her entry into the club and that was her only objective.

After checking her coat, Beth forced her gaze around the room. She was pleased to see exactly what she had expected—a den of debauchery. So much skin. Asscheeks and breasts were visible in such abundance and were being shown with such pride. She envied those who could so easily display their bodies for all to see, even bodies that weren't perfect.

The air was thick with flowery perfume, cologne, sweat, leather and the scent of sex—faint but still detectable. She squeezed through the masses of people, brushing up against warm and soft skin and reveling in the intimacy of it all. She chose the darkest corner she could find, perched herself on a stool and studied the room.

A few men circled her. She paid them no attention, and they got the hint and moved on. Her sole purpose tonight was to watch. She wasn't there to get laid. She'd fuck herself when she got home. An internal heat was already building within her. Her clit was engorged and rubbing pleasantly against her panties with each shift of her legs.

Her gaze darted from one person or scene to the next, soaking it all in. There was too much to see, too many people to watch kissing, petting, grabbing or spanking.

The thumping music was far too loud but served its purpose. The dance floor moved in an undulating mass of people shifting together to the music. One couple in particular stood out amongst the crowd. The woman was the most magnificent beauty Beth had ever seen. She had presence and the ability to dominate a room simply by being in it.

The woman's school mistress costume was well put together—her figure was beautifully accentuated in a black leather skirt, fitted blouse, fishnet hose, and black shiny boots. She wore black-framed glasses and her curly hair was piled on her head in a sexy up-do. Her partner's outfit wasn't nearly as inspired, but Beth wasn't paying him much attention anyway. It was his hands she was watching. His hands roamed over the globes of his partner's ass with a confidence that was intensely striking.

She was fixated on them. Song after song, the couple swayed together in a dance of seduction. She imagined them together in bed, and wondered if the heat they had together here translated the same when they fucked. Her pussy tensed at the thought.

"Hi."

"Huh?"

She immediately resented the intrusion. A man was crouched down beside her. She barely glanced at him.

"Can I offer you a foot massage?"

She returned her gaze to the dance floor. The couple had moved and she spotted them walking away.

"No thanks."

She moved through throngs of people standing together in clusters of twos, threes and fours. She followed the couple down the stairs but lost sight of them at the bottom while trying to squeeze through people coming up. Her gaze scanned the crowd and she caught sight of them going down a hallway she hadn't noticed before. Standing in front of the doors, Beth turned to look behind her. The hallway was empty. She got closer to the women's bathroom door. She heard faint giggling from within. She burst through the door, went to a stall, sat down and peed. She heard nothing from the stall beside her. She flushed, washed her hands, hit the button for the hand dryer, and stood for what seemed like a reasonable amount of time. Then she stepped back from the door, opened it, but let it close without stepping through.

Beth was quick on her feet and heading back into the stall, moving up on tiptoes to avoid the sound of her clicking heels. Conveniently, the stall doors went nearly to the ground, thereby hiding her feet. She stepped up on the toilet just as the dryer clicked off. She crouched there, frozen in space, fearful of moving.

"We're alone," the woman said from the next stall.

Her heart was beating madly in her chest, her stomach felt jittery and nervous. Her panties were moist against her cunt and not nearly tight enough to stop the trail of liquid she could feel tickling her inner thigh as it descended down her skin.

Their kissing sounded hot and frenzied, their breathing labored and passionate. The sound of clothing being unzipped punctuated the near quiet of the room.

"Are you going to fuck me here, lover?" the woman hissed at him.

"Yeah. Suck my cock first," he answered, his voice harsh and demeaning. Evidently her disciplinarian outfit was nothing more than a costume.

Beth eased herself up, her legs shaking with the effort to keep quiet. She peered over the top of the stall. The couple had picked the largest corner stall, big enough to easily fit them both.

The woman was sinking down to her knees. His fly was already open and his cock stood erect in his hand. He was looking down at her, watching her mouth envelop his cock. And what a thing of beauty it was, watching this woman's scarlet-colored lips settle around his cock and suck the length of it.

Beth's fingers found their way to her blouse and undid the top buttons. She slid her hand inside, pushed her bra aside and pinched her nipple.

The man's eyes were closed with his head leaning back against the wall, his hands resting on the woman's head, lightly caressing her hair. She was stunning, her darkened eyelids closed while she took nearly the entire length of him in her mouth. One hand was wrapped around the base of his cock while the other stroked and fingered his balls and it appeared she was teasing his asshole.

Beth's cunt was wanton now. The heat between her legs was traveling down her thighs and up her stomach. Her armpits felt damp and her forehead was glazed with a thin film of sweat. Trying hard to maintain her balance she slipped her hand into her panties. The crotch was saturated. Her fingers were frantic, moving from her clit to her slit, dipping a few fingers inside and back again.

"Fuck! That feels so good," the man said. The man had started moving his hips to meet the woman's mouth. Her eyes snapped open and looked up at him. Beth jerked her head away from the ledge too quickly and nearly stumbled. She'd been seen. The woman had caught the movement above her. Their eyes had connected.

Beth froze, her hand still in her panties, her fingers on her nipple.

"Come here and watch," the woman said.

Beth remained frozen.

"Come here and watch," she repeated.

Hesitantly, Beth again peered over the edge. The man's eyes were open now and looking up at her. He smiled. The woman was unfazed, eyes closed and still sucking him.

Beth stepped down from her perch, out of her stall and into theirs. She squeezed past their bodies and pressed herself into the corner. She might as well not have been there for all they cared. The man glanced at Beth's open shirt.

"Keep going," he said to her before closing his eyes.

Beth reached under her skirt and pulled her panties down to pool around her ankles. With her hand back in her shirt and her fingers stroking herself she again fixed her eyes on the couple.

"Stop. I'll cum," the man snarled.

The woman stood up and held Beth's stare as she hiked her skirt up around her waist, revealing a black lace thong. Faint pink lines of upraised skin blemished the flesh of her ass. If she had been flogged or caned earlier in the night Beth regretted that she had missed the show.

"You like to watch?" the woman asked.

"Yessss…" Beth purred as she continued stroking herself.

"You'll enjoy this then."

The man grabbed at his partner's panties and tore them down her thighs, grabbed her by the wrists, spun her around and pushed her up against the wall. She was slick between her legs, her shaven pussy lips glistening in the light.

Bent slightly with her ass tilted in the air, the woman was a vision to behold. Beth's fingers worked harder on her own clit as she watched him sink his cock into the other woman's pink-ness, spreading her lips wide. He wrapped his arm around her waist and went to work on her clit, his fingers easily sliding over her nub with her juices.

"My ass. Please," the woman begged.

Beth was near cumming. Her cunt was on fire, her pussy and fingers dripping with her juices.

The man moistened his fingers and thumb with the woman's juices, gently circled her anus and pushed a finger inside. His other thrusting was unrelenting; he was pulling his cock near-ly all the way out and sinking it back into her up to his balls. Beth's fingers matched his rhythm on her clit while she finger-fucked herself in unison with him.

"Harder. Please," the woman said.

Beth didn't think it possible for him to fuck her any harder, although he managed. He thrust harder and faster, the muscles of his ass contracting with the effort.

Immense pressure was building within Beth's cunt. She stroked her clit harder. An orgasm ripped through her sex and felt like it would split her in two. She plunged her fingers deeper. She sank to her knees, unable to support herself on her shaking legs. Wave after wave of aftershock passed through her as she fixed her gaze on his cock plunging into his partner, his finger still buried in the woman's ass.

The woman appeared close to cumming, her face awash in pleasure.

"Come on, little girl," he commanded her, slowing his rhythm and burying another finger in her ass. His grip tightened harder around her waist as a series of orgasms ripped through her. She grimaced, moaned and bucked, pushing herself harder onto his cock. He was quick to follow, pumping and emptying his seed into her, pulling out and leaving a line of cum to run down her legs.

"Thank you," Beth whispered from her crouched spot on the floor.

She stood up on quivering legs and pulled up her panties with wet fingers.

"You're welcome," the man said.

The woman grabbed toilet paper and wiped herself clean while the man pulled up his boxers and pants.

After washing her hands Beth thanked the couple again and left the bathroom. On her way out of the club she was handed a pass to the next show.

"What's the theme next time?" she asked.

"Angels and devils," she was told.

"Thanks."

Beth mentally perused her wardrobe on the walk to her car. She was sure she could come up with an appropriate costume. Her need had been satisfied, at least for a little while. Now she eagerly anticipated finding herself watching once again the following month.

STRANGERS IN THE WATER

R. Gay

I owe my existence to the frantic coupling
of two strangers in 1937 in the shallow and
bloody waters of the Massacre River that sep-
arates Haiti from the Dominican Republic.
The story of this incident is told in hushed,
awkward tones, on those rare occasions it is
told at all, as if it is we who must bear shame
for the indiscretion of my grandparents. My
mother never speaks of it. She tries to distance
herself from the geography of so much pain,
and now, only travels to Haiti when absolutely necessary. It is not that she is ashamed of
her mother, or the circumstances of her birth,
but to imagine her mother and a stranger fleeing the Dominican Republic and hiding in the
waters of the river while soldiers slaughtered
people on both banks, only to seek solace in

each other, reminds her of a history she only wants to forget. Perhaps it is a history we all want to forget. But every morning when she stares in the mirror, or when she catches her reflection in a storefront, she is forced to remember.

I am fascinated by this story—this moment of desperation and conception. I asked my grandmother about it once, when my husband Todd and I were in Haiti for a few weeks. I remember how she stared at me with milky eyes, and her small hands, scarred from working in sugarcane fields in Dajabon, the first town across the Dominican border, holding her glass of rum and water so tightly I thought the glass would splinter. I took the glass from her, told her that she had almost hurt herself. She looked away and whispered, "Scars cannot bleed."

Todd and I have been married for three years, together for over six. My mother refers to him as "Mr. America," because in her mind, he represents the wholesome American image she has come to resent. We met at the University of Nebraska, but after our twins were born, I insisted we move to Washington D.C. because if we stayed in that cold, remote place, our little brown babies would always be more mine than his. I try to explain to Todd what it means to be Haitian but it's hard for him to understand that there are places in the world where power outages are commonplace, and the majority of the population wallows in poverty—where no matter how rich or poor you are, you want the same thing, an end to the chaos, a breath of fresh air, a moment of peace. It is hard for him to understand why I would want to be in that place. But it is hard for me to understand why I would want to be anywhere else.

My husband and I have been to Haiti together twice. The first time, he brought a case of bottled water, and found it inexplicable that I wouldn't speak to him for a week afterward.

The second time, he brought ten bottles of mosquito spray. Every night, we would swelter beneath the mosquito netting of our bed, and when we tried to make love, he made me nauseous with the aerosol stench of insect repellant.

Then, upon our return to the airport in Miami, he kissed the ground, and was subject to two weeks of the silent treatment. For the sake of our relationship, we keep international travel to a minimum. But now I have this need to go to Haiti, because it is the only place in the world that truly feels like home. My grandmother is getting older, the country is getting worse, and if I don't go now, the places I remember, the people that make it home, will no longer be there. My grandmother lives in Ouanaminthe, the first town on the Haitian side of the Massacre River. I don't understand why she chooses to live so close to a place of horror but sometimes I think that she can't bear to part with the memories, as if the further away she gets from that place, the more she will forget. Her house is a small, cement affair. There are palm trees in the front yard and a small iron gate to ward off unwanted visitors. She often sits on her porch, staring toward the river, a distant look in her eyes. When she's like this, I can only watch her. A silence surrounds her that demands respect.

She and my grandfather worked on a plantation in Dajabon, cutting sugarcane. They didn't know each other, but they didn't need to. They shared the same condition. I have heard the stories of cane workers—days beneath a tormenting sun, cruel overseers, little pay, a life much like the slaves in America. I cannot imagine what it must have been like for my grandmother, a small woman in a big world that she could not hope to understand. When General Rafael Trujillo ordered all Haitians out of the Dominican Republic, she gathered her few belongings and wrapped them in her skirt. She ran from the overseers, and people throwing stones and marauding soldiers only to find more soldiers on both sides of the river. She found a shallow place and even beneath the moonlight, she could see that the water ran red with blood. The water was icy cold and as she waded in, a body floated past her. She waited, her heart stopping every time she saw the barrel of a soldier's rifle or heard the heavy footsteps of military boots plodding along damp soil. She heard the screams of men, women, and children being slaughtered, the thrashing of limbs in water, the silence of death.

She closed her eyes and thought about her childhood, the sound of her mother singing, the smell of fresh laundry, her father's paintings. She didn't notice when a large man slipped into the water. She couldn't scream when he tapped her shoulder. She wanted to tell him to go away—that two were easier to spot than one, but she looked into his eyes and saw her fear mirrored there. As she lay in the water shivering, the small part of her heart still remaining opened up, and she wrapped her arms around this stranger. For hours, but perhaps it was only minutes, they lay there holding each other until she could feel his heart beating against hers, every breath of his followed by one of hers until she was certain that they were breathing for each other.

She did not protest when she felt his cold lips pressed against hers. She opened her mouth and felt respite at the warmth she found in his. His large hands unbuttoned her blouse, covered her breasts. They lifted her skirt, and turned her onto her back and held her as he entered her swiftly. He buried his face in her neck. She buried her face in his shoulder. With each thrust, the coarse fabric of his shirt scraped her cheek. She felt a tightening between her thighs. His chest seemed to hollow as he sobbed silently. Even after they came, he remained inside her. He remained inside her until young shafts of morning light gave witness to the carnage around them. Only then did he withdraw and steal home, as silently as he had crept into the water.

She saw him again, later that day. His name was Jean-Marc. He was neither handsome nor ugly but from his demeanor, she decided that he was a good man. At first, they pretended not to recognize each other, but then he smiled a sad little smile, and again, her heart opened up. He reached for her hand and she brushed his fingertips with hers. He took her to get warm clothing, a bit of food. She would have married him, my grandmother told me, but he was killed three weeks later as he snuck back into the Dominican Republic to find his younger sister. When she found out that my grandfather had died, she wanted to cry, she wanted to scream, she wanted to throw herself in the river but instead, she found work as a maid with a well-to-do family. She gave birth to my mother. She finally did cry when she saw her daughter, an exact likeness of the man she knew but for a moment. And then she hoped to never cry again. Instead, she lived as close to the river as her heart would allow, and talked to the waters as if they held the spirit of Jean-Marc.

There are no pictures of my grandfather. Sometimes, when I think of my grandmother's story, I imagine him, tall and strong, proud. I imagine the times he and my grandmother should have had, and when I do this, I cry the tears my grandmother cannot. There is no explanation for this. It is as if my grandmother's grief skipped a generation and now resides in me. And her grief is a burden I did not ask for, but one I bear.

The tears I cry for her, for Jean-Marc, are yet another thing Todd cannot understand. He knows the story, as he was there when my grandmother told us her saga and I believe that he truly mourns the tragedy, but he mourns it the way he mourns other atrocities—from a comfortable distance—a distance I cannot nor will not share.

My mother disapproves of my going back to Haiti. "Nothing good will come of it," she told me. "And it's not safe." But nothing good will come of not going, either. Just as Todd cannot understand certain parts of me, I cannot understand certain parts of my mother. I cannot understand her unwillingness to go home, but perhaps it is that her memories are stained with a different, more paralyzing brand of grief that holds her where she is. At the airport, she hugs me tightly, and I can feel wetness against my chest when she pulls away. She stuffs a thick envelope into my hand, orders me to give it to her mother, not to open it. I beg her to come with us, but she shakes her head, hides behind a dark pair of sunglasses, grips the handles of the twins' stroller, the veins in her hands pulsing. As we head into the airplane, I think I hear her calling after us.

After we make it through customs, Todd and I are standing in front of the airport waiting for a cab. I am already irritated with him, and the expression on his face. The air is heavy, thick enough that it takes effort to breathe. In the distance, we can see black plumes of smoke filtering through the sky as political dissenters burn tires. Cabdrivers lean against their cars, sucking their teeth, inspecting passengers as they try to deduce who will pay the most for their services. At once, things are silent and loud, still and frenetic. It is a scene that can only be found here on my island. Todd is sweating, his tie hanging loose around his neck. His nose is wrinkled, as if he can't quite place a distinct and unpleasant odor. I pinch the soft skin beneath his elbow and he winces.

"Why did you do that?"

"Stop looking like that."

"Like what?"

I bite my lower lip. "Never you mind."

A cabdriver finally decides we'll pay him enough, and throws our bags into the trunk of his beaten Mercedes. Todd and I climb into the backseat, and as the car lurches toward downtown Port-Au-Prince, we hold each other's hands so tightly, I can no longer feel my fingers.

Driving in Haiti is a peculiar thing. There seems to be no reason nor rhyme as to how fast people drive, where in the road people drive, or any other traffic rules I am accustomed to in the States. By the time we arrive at the Hotel Montana, where we will be staying for a night before heading to Ouanaminthe, Todd looks peaked. I forgive him the heavy sigh of relief he exhales as he shoves a few dollars into the driver's hands.

Our room is rather bare, but well appointed. This hotel, it seems, is one of the nicer ones in town. But the towels, though clean, are worn. The cakes of soap in the bathroom are so thin, it's a wonder how anyone could properly bathe himself. The bed is old and small, and the air-conditioning coughs on our sweaty skin ever so faintly. Todd takes a shower, and I lie on the bed, naked and waiting for him. It has been a long day for both of us. I wish my mother were here. I don't like not having a clear understanding of why I am here. I'm hoping that I won't regret the decision to bring my husband along. But nonetheless, I am glad Todd is here, because he is home and Haiti is home and I want to savor the experience of these two homes together.

When he comes out of the bathroom, all the steam from the bathroom enters the room and the air thickens. I can literally feel sweat covering my skin. Todd smiles shyly, and my lingering irritation disappears as lightly as a whisper. He lets the towel around his waist fall to the floor and crawls into bed, atop me, his damp skin clinging to mine. His cock is hard, momentarily resting against my left thigh before he is inside me and we're struggling to move against each other but already, I feel sharp spirals of pleasure working their way up my legs. We make love so quickly that afterward I can hardly believe that we've even touched. Todd falls asleep first, but I lie awake, staring at the cracks in the ceiling, wondering about the sound of my grandfather's voice.

We wake early the next morning, and through the dirty window we can see that the sky is still dark with plumes of smoke. We take breakfast in our room—mangos, toast and cheese. And then we sit, bags packed as if we are afraid to move forward from this point. I call my mother, assure her that things are fine but I can hear the doubt in her voice. Perhaps I hear the doubt in mine. Finally Todd stands up.

"We'd best get going."

I smile. "Yes. My grandparents are waiting for us."

Todd looks confused, but he gets our bags and soon we are driving on what passes for roads, toward Ouanaminthe. We pass mile after mile of sugarcane fields and dark sweaty men stare at us as we pass by, sucking their lower lips, machetes paused in midair and you can tell that they'd rather strike themselves than one more stalk of cane. And then their machetes fall as if they are thinking, next time, next time I'll have the courage. Working in cane fields is brutal, bitter work. Men and even women spend twelve hours a day beneath the unforgiving island sun, as their skin is shredded by the brambles about. My grandmother has told me stories of how she used to tend to her friends' wounds as they lay on the dirt floor of the servant quarters late at night, using a poultice and strips of old clothing to hold back blood and infection. She would tell me of the guilt she felt when she was moved from the fields to the master's house; watching her friends from the comfort of a kitchen or sitting room window, and then the relief of no longer having to toil alongside them. It is strange—so many years later, very little has changed in the cane fields of this island.

When we arrive in Ouanaminthe, that sense of anticipation is gone. There is not much to see here. It is a small town that looks like most towns in this part of the country; in every part of the country. The houses are worn cement blocks, all the windows open. There is a small market with a sad array of wares, a few bars, and other shops. And on a small dirt road so close to the water that I can taste the Massacre River in my mouth, there is my grandmother's house surrounded by a black iron fence. For some reason, I expect to see her standing in the dust of her front yard, but her lot is empty, save for the coconut trees, standing naked, skeletons of fertility.

As we park in the small driveway and close the gate behind us, my grandmother appears in the doorway and I gasp, gripping Todd's hand. As his fingers curl around mine, it feels like they are wrapping around my heart, holding it safe. Looking at my grandmother reminds me of the trees in her yard; she looks like a ghost of the woman I knew growing up, of the woman I saw in the black-and-white photos in my mother's albums. But her eyes, a deep blue, shine as she drinks me in, cautiously steps toward us. When she opens her arms, I know exactly what she looked like as a younger woman; what she looked like before grief formed a home in her features.

She leads us into the house and we sit at a small Formica table, cracked and wobbly. In the center of the table is a pitcher of lemonade and three clean glasses. She pours for Todd first, then me, and finally herself before sitting down. I remove my mother's envelope from my backpack and slide it across the table to my grandmother, whose eyes water as she traces the edges of the envelope with one knotted finger.

"Your mother couldn't come?"

It is less of a question, more a statement of fact. I shake my head, and gently cover my grandmother's hand with mine. "She stayed behind to watch the twins." Beneath the table, I nudge Todd's knee with mine, and he pulls their pictures from his wallet, smiling proudly as he lays them on the table.

"Miriam," my grandmother whispers.

I smile, but there are tears streaming down my cheeks and I don't quite understand why. "Jean-Marc and Sebastien; we named them Jean-Marc and Sebastien."

She nods slowly; swollen arcs of tears rest on her lower eyelids. "They look like your grandfather." She turns her head to the side, toward the river, and rests the palm of her hand against her breastbone. "Yes. They look like your grandfather."

I can only take her word for this. The only images of this man in my mind are pieced together from years of my grandmother's stories—the same stories repeated over and over as if to tell a few stories many times will take the place of the life she and my grandfather did not have, stories she should have had. I study the pictures of my children and all of a sudden I miss them. I've been so wrapped up in being home and not understanding why I'm here that I haven't had time to miss their sweet and sour breath, their coos, their chubby hands and feet. I want to bring them here, when the time is right, when we can look at the Port-au-Prince skyline and not see smoke, when we can walk down the street and now worry about the children being kidnapped for ransom. Everyone here thinks Americans are rich. In many ways, they are right. But I don't want my children to be victims of that fact. I want that perfect time to be sooner than later. And I want my mother here as well, so that we will be four generations of my family standing on our native soil. I want a lot of things. It is the nature of my people to want things we do not know how to have.

Until Todd and I started visiting Haiti, I hadn't been here since I was ten years old. Back then, we came to Haiti every summer but that last visit was special, almost idyllic. We were sheltered from the island's truths. My father shimmed up coconut trees, his pants rolled up his thin calves, and threw down coconuts that my mother cracked open with a machete. We ate *douce*, a kind of Haitian fudge, until our lips shriveled in protest. My brothers and I swam and stared at each other under water, marveling that there was water on this earth clearer than anything we had ever seen. One day, while my mother shopped in the city, my dad took us away to La Citadel, a fort, and as we climbed and climbed and climbed, my father told us stories of warriors and freedom and I knew that this was the happiest I would ever see him. I remember thinking how much cooler my parents were in Haiti than back in the States.

And then they took us to Ouanaminthe, and as we approached the town, all the smiles and laughter disappeared and in a far too brief moment, I thought I might never remember what my parents looked like when they were happy.

My mother fidgeted in her seat, my father gripped the steering wheel so tightly his knuckles turned white, and my brothers and I sat nervous and knobby-kneed, trying to understand why all of a sudden, things were so different.

There was my grandmother, who smelled like lavender and rum and spoiled us rotten with sweets and attention and long walks. But then she and my mother would disappear for hours at a time. We were under strict orders not to follow them. We'd pester my father for an explanation, but he would brush us off, look toward the river, then distract us by carving puppets or telling us more stories. Finally on the second to last day of our visit, my father lay down with my brothers for a nap, and left to my own devices, I was determined to find my mother. I set out through the gate and followed the trickling sound of water until I reached the banks of the Massacre River. I knew nothing about the river, then, but I saw a bridge in the distance, and I saw soldiers and rifles. It was just like something in a movie. And there, maybe twenty feet from where I was standing, were my mother and grandmother, kneeling as they ran their fingers through the water. Their lips were moving but I couldn't hear them. I walked toward them, but they didn't notice me until I was standing next to them, and even then, I had to clear my throat. When they looked up at the same time, I remember thinking that they looked like paper dolls because their profiles were so alike. And I remember that they were crying—their eyes were red like blood—their eyes were so red that I could not recognize them as women who gave me life, women who loved me. The sight of them scared me so much that I ran back to my grandmother's house and crawled into bed with my father, resting my head against his chest so I could smell his cologne and hear the beating of his heart. We never spoke of that moment, and the next day as we drove away, I stared at my grandmother's figure through the rear window and she had that same look in her eyes—hollow, desperate, lonely.

The first few days of my visit with my grandmother pass without event. We talk about the children and my parents and my brothers and my job. When Todd is exploring the town, mixing with the natives, as he calls it, we talk about him. My grandmother likes him, his simplicity, the tenderness he shows me. She says you can trust a man who looks at a woman the way he looks at me. She says my grandfather looked at her that way. When I ask her what way, she sucks her teeth and looks at me with disgust. "You," she tells me. "You are in many ways like your mother. You take the things around you for granted."

At night, Todd and I lie beneath mosquito netting, our bodies damp and heavy. "Is it always like this?" he asks.

"It's an island."

"Seriously."

I sigh. "Haiti has always been hot, will always be hot. I don't question it and thinking hard right now would just make me hotter."

Todd chuckles. "I can think of a more enjoyable way to make you hotter." He traces a line from my chin to my navel, and gently nibbles my earlobe, but I push him away.

"It's too hot for that sort of thing."

"It's never too hot."

"Then this will teach you a lesson about never saying never." I can feel him pull away in the darkness. I don't need to see his face to know that he is pouting. I thought I would feel closer to him, being here with him, but mostly I am annoyed by his presence. He is keeping me from what I should really be doing, whatever that is.

"Maybe it was a mistake for me to come," he says.

"I wanted you to be here," I whisper. I know I don't sound convincing.

"What you wanted and what really is are two different things. I feel like you're expecting something of me without telling me what that something is."

I turn away from him, wrapping my arms around myself. "I'm tired. Go to sleep."

I lie perfectly still and pretend to fall asleep until I hear his snoring. My slumber is punctuated by a torment of slain bodies and cruel soldiers with white, freakishly large teeth and the husks of small children floating in massacred water.

The next morning, Todd wakes up before me, and when I stumble into the kitchen, he and my grandmother are sitting at the table drinking coffee. He refuses to look at me, but I kiss him on the forehead and sit down, rubbing my eyes.

"You look like you had a terrible sleep," my grandmother says.

"Bad dreams."

"There are no other kinds in this place."

To hear the resignation in her voice only saddens me. I am overwhelmed by her hopelessness, by the hopelessness I see in the faces of the men and women and children all around me. I spend the day with my grandmother. When she goes to the river to talk to my grandfather, I go with her and she doesn't protest. Instead, we walk together and we are silent, but again her lips are moving, as if she is filling him in on our visit, his great-grandchildren, the details of her life. In my mind, I talk to him too. I ask him if he ever found his sister, if it was worth all this pain to go back for her. I ask him to send my grandmother some sign that he actually hears her. The river is much smaller now than it was then; it is more a stream than anything else. The soldiers are still there, but they hardly pay attention to anything other than their gossip and the cigarettes they smoke. The river is still shallow and dark and when I run my fingers through the water, it is a frightening kind of cold that demands escape. I can hardly imagine it, the people fleeing, thrashing through midnight waters, dead bodies floating to the surface, the water running red. But I can hear echoes of their screams as the water runs around rocks and a child splashes about under the watchful eye of her mother. When my grandmother and I finally look at each other, I wonder if I look the way my mother did when I stumbled upon them so many years ago.

I leave my grandmother there with her memories. It is clear she needs to be alone. Todd is nowhere to be found so I crawl into bed and wait for the cool of night. Later, when it seems that the entire world is asleep, I awake and Todd is beside me, wrapped around the edge of the bed. I shake his shoulder and he turns to me.

"Is something wrong?" he asks, groggily.

I press my finger against his lips, hand him his shorts, and motion for him to follow me. It is an eerily quiet night. It is darker than a night ever could be back in America.

"Where are we going?" he asks.

I shake my head and we keep walking until we are at the river. I step into the water and look up at my husband. "My grandfather died here. Thousands of people died here. But my mother was also conceived here. Strange, isn't it, that this river is both a place of death and life?"

"Yes," Todd says. "It's such a small river."

"I thought the same thing this morning."

He nods, rubbing his eyes. "Why are we here?"

I pull my T-shirt up and over my head, tossing it onto the riverbank before stepping out of my shorts. I stand naked before him. Then I lower myself into the water, and gasp.

"What are you doing?" Todd whispers, loudly.

"Come here."

He looks around nervously and in the pause I feel terribly alone. I now understand why my grandparents did what they did, anchoring themselves to each other.

"Please."

He wades into the water. I can feel the silt of the riverbed beneath my body. It has a life of its own as it works its way around my elbows and into the small of my back.

"Take your clothes off."

"I don't know about this, Miriam. What if we get caught?"

"We won't," I promise.

There is doubt in his eyes, but he strips quickly and squats, shivering. I lie back and giggle as the water tickles me. I can feel my hair fanning out. Suddenly, it is as if Todd realizes what I need him to do. He crawls atop me and I sink lower into the river, until only the tips of my breasts and my nipples are above water. The muscles in my neck are aching slightly as I hold my head up. He brushes his lips along the sharp of my collarbone and I look at him, once again marveling at how pale he is compared to me. Shadows from nearby trees are cast across our bodies. The night is ever so still. I don't really feel like I'm here. In my mind, it is 1937 and I am cold, afraid, and hungry for this man atop me to commit the act of touch. I clasp the back of Todd's neck with my hand and press my lips against his, so hard that they become numb. He forces his tongue between my lips—he tastes salty and there is rum on his breath. His fingers press into my shoulders. There will be bruises in the morning. I wrap one leg around his waist and wince as small rocks cut into my back. The water is colder now. I close my eyes for a moment and when I open them, the water is red, almost as warm as blood. I hear screams in the near distance. At once I am alone and with Todd and surrounded by ghosts. He covers my mouth with his other hand and my head sinks into the water. My eyes burn. The water tastes sanguine.

My husband makes love to me in a slow steady rhythm, and I pull him deeper and deeper into me until I'm certain that our bodies will remain forever joined like this. Cool water and soft silt slide beneath me and I begin moving my hips, forcing myself against Todd, urging him to fuck me harder. I want this to hurt. I want to remember him like this, fucking me in the river, tomorrow when I am sitting. He nestles his chin in the space between my shoulder and my neck.

"I don't understand what's happening," he says, hoarsely.

I don't have any answers for him.

I can't stop crying. I cry enough tears to fill this Massacre River—tears for my grandmother who cannot forget, who will never feel what I am feeling in this moment and in every moment after; for my mother who pretends she has forgotten; for myself, and the burden of this country's grief. I scream into his hand. I hate that this feels so good but I don't want to stop. The sound of his body splashing against mine overwhelms me. When I look at him, I hardly recognize him. His jaw is set with determination, his eyes are almost vacant. I let my head fall underwater and then he looks hazy, like an apparition. My chest tightens but I remain submerged. I allow myself to drown. In this moment, the ghosts of these waters will breathe for me.

Todd is saying something to me, but I cannot hear him. My ears are filled with water and memory. I begin to shake and as I rise for air, my hair plastered against my face, I throw my arms back, and the upper half of my body floats. I look up and see the moon. My body shudders violently until I feel so much pain and pleasure at once that it is unbearable. I have to push him away from me. We stare at each other and for a moment, we too are strangers in these waters. And then his arms are wrapped around me, and he is leading me onto land. I know why I needed to be here.

UNICORN SIGHTING

Lola David

A few men lingered outside as we walked in. They waited, presumably watching through the heavily tinted glass doors, to see if we were buying tickets. I glanced backward as J moved to the counter. You could almost see their faces pressed near the glass, or eyes peeking through the doors that hadn't yet closed all the way.

Inside, it felt like an abandoned movie theatre, suspended in time. The orange and purple paisley carpet had seen better days and more savory clients. Frameless posters hung on the dingy rust-colored walls. VHS covers of buxom, big-haired blondes cluttered what used to be a refreshment counter. I'd have liked to have seen some hand sanitizer and condoms in those cabinets. But, that's just me.

"Two tickets?" J asked. He offered the man

behind the counter forty dollars, but the man gingerly plucked only one twenty dollar bill from J's hand.

"She's free," he said under his breath, gesturing to me.

J held me close, his arm around my waist, and ushered me into the theatre. He could already feel the eyes on us. And I felt only slightly better with him there.

Two men standing at the doorway held back the vinyl-lined doors for us. The theatre was long, narrow and completely black save for the girl-on-girl porn on-screen. Thank god for the glaring white background behind the girls. We could at least make out heads to find a seat several rows from the back. We'd have tucked ourselves into the back row, but it looked and sounded fairly occupied.

I could count. There were at least thirty heads scattered about the recesses of the theatre. Some sat closer to the center at precise distances away from other patrons. Two or three seats, at the least, separated most of the heady silhouettes.

I felt like we could get mobbed at any moment. I wasn't comfortable. I'm not sure what I expected, having never been here before. But it was the last week that this theatre would be open. The neighbors had finally pressured the city into rezoning for condominiums. J and I wanted to be able to at least say that we'd been there "back in the day."

Thinking back I can't remember why were stupid enough to get a seat in the middle of the seventh row from the back. We should have been looking for something with a quick exit— an aisle seat. Anywhere would have been better. Our initial thought was to be away from the figures lurking in the dark recesses of the back rows, sides and corners.

We sat down and I slid my coat off. J and I sat there a little stiffly first. The sound of Ginger Lynn's orgasm was just quiet enough that you could hear the friction of hand on flesh and the movement of clothing in a repetitive, smooth motion—back and forth. It echoed rapidly in some corners and slower in others. We could hear them holding their breaths and then gasping as they got closer to coming. There was one man in the very front of the theatre who didn't give a damn who heard him moan as he came. The theatre reeked of musky sweat and semen.

The thought of all of those men in that room with different fantasies, conquests, sluts, and fetishes was decadent. My mind raced. I was intimidated and aroused, all at the same time.

I reached between J's legs and started rubbing him through his pants. I could feel him harden quickly.

Two more men entered the theatre, presumably the ones lurking outside when we came in. The huskier of the two sat directly in front of us. The other sat in our row, at the aisle closest to me.

I looked at J briefly—a "should we get the fuck out of here?" look.

He leaned to my ear. I was ready to bolt as soon as he gave the word. But he knows too well how to calm me.

"Kiss me," he breathed.

He turned my face to him without waiting for my response. My lips met his gently. I let his whiskers tickle my lips before I pressed into him. He inhaled deeply and our kiss grew deeper. His tongue moved gracefully under mine. His lips still guided my movement. His hands drifted down to my dress that wrapped and tied at the side of my waist. He slid his hand in to cup my breast as he kissed me. His whiskers grazed my neck and shoulder, sending chills down my spine.

But without him at my lips, my gaze wandered around us. The man at the end of my aisle was now three seats from me.

I could feel the presence of two more men behind us. I dared not look. As my anxiety increased, J pulled back my bra and exposed my breast. I gasped from the shock and the chill of the room. He cradled the weight of my breast in his hand and let the intermittent brightness of the film flash off of my white flesh.

How many eyes were on me—my breast? Should we continue? If any more of my flesh was exposed I might suddenly have strange hands all over my body. It would be a thrill, but ungoverned it could be overwhelming. Overwhelming for J. God, I wished we had at least one familiar body with us tonight. He'd be sitting to my right as a buffer, to be sure.

The men disappeared from my mind again as soon as I felt J start licking and tugging at my nipple. I moaned again, and laced my fingers in his hair. It was my turn to guide him. He bit at the fleshy curve beneath my nipple. His hand drifted down to lift my skirt and I stopped him.

My eyes were locked on the gaze of the husky man who was in front of us. He was now turned completely around, watching. And the man three seats to my right was now right next to me. His jacket was across his lap, hiding the erection he was stroking.

I squeezed J's hand and, I think, pulled his hair a bit. He sat up.

Do you say "hi?"

We didn't have to. "Are you guys looking for company tonight?"

"Well—" I started.

"No," J said.

"Okay. Well have a great evening. You're stunning," he said to me. The husky one turned back around.

"I'm not done with you yet. Do you trust me?"

"I don't want to go any further with this crowd around us," I whispered.

"I know."

J tapped Husky on the shoulder. "I'm taking her outside to fuck her if you want to watch."

The guy with the jacket next to me heard J and asked if he could watch as well.

"Yes, but keep it to yourself. We'll leave in a moment."

J grabbed my hand. "Are you okay?"

"Yes."

"Good."

J took me outside, Husky and the Jacket following us.

We walked around the back of the theatre where our car was parked. He leaned me up against the car and kissed me again. His lips felt softer than before, waiting for the passion from mine. "Are you okay?"

"Yes."

J turned me around and bent me over the car. All three of them were behind me. J lifted my dress to expose my ass and the black lace garter belt and stockings I had on.

"You are a lucky man," Husky muttered.

J motioned for them both to walk around the front of the car, standing to the side of us. J knelt down, kissing and licking my pussy from behind. I was wet from our play in the theatre. I pushed back against him, suggesting my readiness for his cock.

The Jacket and Husky already had their cocks in hand. I kept my eyes on them as J thrust into me. It was a show, so he pushed hard. I felt the head of his cock painfully deep inside me. Husky and the Jacket muttered something as he fucked me harder and harder. He wound his hand in my hair, pulling me back against him.

Husky damn near doubled over after a few moments and came.

J pushed again into me and I tightened around him. He grabbed my hips to pull me into him harder. With one final deep thrust, he came. He lifted me up off the car and pulled me against him. He pulled back my dress to reveal my breasts to the Jacket.

He teased and played with them, letting one hand wander down to my clit. He held the weight of me against him and rubbed me to orgasm.

The Jacket came.

I pulled my dress back together. J grabbed my hand to leave as Husky said, "We'd love to see you here again. You two draw quite a crowd."

"No, she does," J said.

"You guys want to keep playing tonight?" the Jacket asked.

"Not tonight. I'm taking her home to make love to her."

"I would, too. Hope to see you two again soon...."

ALL THE FLOODGATES
EVER MADE

Miel Rose

I was almost done with the job.

The herb garden was big. It had taken me
more than a week to get it in order. It was a
dream working in such an old and diverse garden. There were huge and beautiful stands of
lavender, wormwood and rosemary, decades
old, and I grew intoxicated surrounded by
their strong fragrances. There were poppies
gone to seed, their pods rattling, broadcast-
ing seed all over the garden. Come spring they
would be everywhere, along with the angelica
and the calendula. Besides the old European
standbys, Mrs. O'Connelly had transplanted a
dozen or more natives from the surrounding
woods and trained them to cultivation. There
was doll eyes with its white berries, each one
with a black spot on the top looking like a

tiny eyeball, and its cousin black cohosh. There was the shiny ground cover of partridge berry, the lacy foliage of bleeding heart, the shocking blue berries of clintonia. There was violet and bloodroot, lobelia and betony. Being a plant lover and an herb nerd, I was head over heels.

I was finishing up painstakingly weeding between the mugwort and the greater celendine, and with a last tug at a dandelion root that had strayed from the area allowed to the taraxacums, I sighed and got up to bring my pile of weeds to the compost.

I'd been called in for this job because no one on Wade's crew knew enough about medicinal plants to handle the herb garden. They'd been hired to help out the elderly couple who lived on this old farmstead. Wade asked me if I'd be interested in weeding a garden that might have been made up entirely of weeds for all they knew about it. Some of the plants were indeed weeds, but interesting ones, and I could tell what was to stay and what was for the compost heap. So, since I was broke and jobless I agreed to come out and whip the garden into shape.

Not that I didn't have my reservations. I make it a policy not to work jobs with people I'm dating. Plus, spending my days working with a bunch of macho dudes wasn't my idea of a good time, even if some of them are like my brothers.

Maybe an outsider would have no idea what I'm talking about, just seeing us as one big happy dyke work crew. The thing is though, I'm a femme. While I have no qualms pulling on my Carhartt overalls as practicality dictates, I still find myself with insecurities about how others perceive my gender when I'm in that mode. Most people's perceptions of gender are so shallow, skin deep indeed. Also, I wasn't looking forward to the typical scenario of having to prove I'm a capable and hard worker just because you mostly see me in a skirt. Borrowing trouble, per usual; working in the garden had been pleasant and solitary with little of the bullshit I had anticipated.

After dumping my weeds in the compost and hosing off my muddy hands, I went off toward the house to check the time. Passing the barn, I saw Wade, pitchfork in hand, walking toward the ladder to the loft. Her T-shirt was dark with sweat and her hair was sticking up in clumps. She turned and saw me, breaking into her crazy-ass grin that more often than not reduces my panties to wetland.

"Good, you finished with the garden just in time to help me pitch the rest of this hay."

"Honey, you know pitching hay isn't in my job description," I said, hand on hip.

"Baby, it's easy. Come on, grab a pitchfork."

Sighing, I grabbed the fork and followed Wade up into the loft. Truth be told, I was tired and I just wanted to go home and take a bath. But there wasn't much hay left anyway, so I got to work pitching it off the loft. I worked steadily for about fifteen minutes before I realized Wade had stopped and was grinning at me, leaning on her pitchfork. I was hot and sweaty and irritation was stronger than any sweet feelings I had for her.

"Don't fucking look at me."

"Why the fuck not?" Her smile did not falter and she threw her pitchfork into the hay.

"I'm here to work, not look sexy for you." I just wanted to get this job done, go home and get cleaned up. I was starting to feel self-conscious in my muddy overalls. I was used to being dressed up and ready for a date when I was around

Wade, and as much as I wished my self-confidence was rock hard and not related to my outfit, it was starting to crumble around the edges.

I stopped working and dropped my fork as Wade started walking toward me. Her eyes had gone flinty and her jaw was clenched, making her muscles stick out from her jawbone. When she reached me she didn't stop, but slowly pushed me backward, helping me navigate the hay piles while giving me a look that sent icy chills down my spine. My back hit the wall and she grabbed my chin with her big, calloused hand.

In her deepest, slowest top voice she said, "I know you. Don't you EVER forget that. I know exactly who you are." She chuckled without cracking the harshness of her expression. "Yeah, like you aren't just as femme in muddy overalls as you are in a skirt and heels."

I guess I was being pretty blatant in my insecurity, but I swear it felt like she was reading my mind.

She turned her head and spit to the side. "That's fucking bullshit. I love that you're a hard worker." Her grin was back, softening the angles of her face, but not quite reaching her eyes. "In fact, watching you has got my dick hard. Too bad I don't have the balls to pack at work."

I felt tears filling my eyes. Her thumb caressed my cheek and her face became tender without losing its intensity. Leaning forward, she kissed me gently, slowly sliding her tongue into my mouth. My knees turned to water and I opened to her, my body relaxing against the barn wall. Her mouth turned to my neck, at first kissing my skin softly with parted, moist lips until I was squirming against her, and then more urgently, using enough suction and teeth to leave me swollen and bruised. Her hand left my jaw and drifted under the bib of my overalls, lifting my tits up and rubbing my nipples in slow firm circles with her thumbs.

Her mouth moved up to my ear and her voice was husky as she said, "I'm going to fuck you."

The spell was broken and I balked. Maybe I could be a good bottom for her in the bedroom, but we were at work, and although no one could see us up here, they could certainly hear us.

"Wade, I don't want to end this job getting caught fucking in Mr. and Mrs. O'Connelly's loft."

"Baby, relax, no one's going to miss us up here."

With a firm grip, she pivoted our bodies sideways and down into the nearest pile of hay. Really, my cunt was wet and swollen already, aching with a dull throb, and with Wade between my legs, grinding into me, my protests were forgotten. Well, almost.

"What if I make too much noise?" I moaned, as she thrust her groin against my canvas-covered pussy.

"I'm not worried about it." She grabbed my arms and held them down above my head and kissed me hard. Then, shifting her grip with one hand holding my wrists, she moved her other hand between us and fumbled to unbutton my fly. A moan escaped my lips and I felt my face arrange itself into the desperate frown of a girl who really needs to get fucked, but is scared of the consequences.

"Baby, relax," she crooned as she saw my face. "How's your pussy?" She slipped her hand through my fly and into my panties, finding my pussy soaking wet and desperate for her fingers. "Jesus Fucking Christ, you're wet." Her eyes closed in rapture and she lowered her head to my chest as she plunged her fingers deep inside me.

I wanted to scream my head off, but instead babbled a stream of quiet pleadings, "Yes, yes, fuck me, fuck me. Harder, baby, please? Harder? You feel so good baby, your fingers are so good, so good. Don't stop, don't stop."

Her grip tightened on my wrists and she groaned in my ear, saying, "Yeah, baby, tell me you like it, that's right, give it to me." She raised her head and looked into my eyes and said, "I'm going to make you cum."

Now, I don't cum when I get fucked, and maybe it's like Wade says, it's because I'm scared and stop her before she brings me there. All I know is that there gets to be this point when what I'm feeling is so intense I can't tell if it's pleasure or pain and yeah, I guess I get scared. It's just too much.

Well, up in that hayloft Wade was quickly taking me to that threshold and it became obvious she meant to push me over. She was gripping my wrists so tightly that I was losing circulation and she was looking deep in my eyes with so much intensity that I knew all I had to do was say the word and she would stop.

I didn't. My pussy felt like it was going to burst into flames from the friction going on inside me. I was so wet and she was fucking me so hard I could hear her fingers pounding in and out of me. That intense pressure was building and I was worried I was going to lose it, lose control, the feeling was too big. I was getting scared, but Wade just kept on fucking me relentlessly, like her arm wasn't about to fall off. She just kept going, fucking her fingers in and out of my wet, sopping pussy while this feeling built inside me, some huge wave set on breaking down all the floodgates ever made.

Wade's eyes were locked on mine and I was staring back in defiance, letting her know I was right there with her, daring her to push me a little further. And she did, her fucking becoming more focused, concentrated.

Her hand left my wrists and clamped down on my mouth right as I was about to start screaming. The wave of feeling broke and maybe I was going to drown in it. This was not like the orgasms I was used to. My body seized up in a round of intense spasms, my pussy clamping down hard on her fingers.

"That's right, girl. Cum for me, baby. Give it to me. You're doing so good. Just a little more, baby, give me a little more. Good girl, that's it." Wade's fingers kept stroking inside me, stretching out my orgasm, riding the waves. My hands, newly released, were holding Wade's hand clamped down over my mouth and I bit into her palm trying to keep this ungodly banshee wailing that was coming through my throat from leaving my mouth. I took a deep breath and whimpered against her palm, kissing the indentations left by my teeth. My muscles relaxed and Wade moved her fingers in slow circles against the walls of my cunt, making me jump and clamp down on her again.

I was so lost in the feeling that it took me a minute to realize I was soaking wet, way more so than I had been minutes ago. It felt like I had ejaculated about a pint of come into my overalls. When my pussy finally stopped contracting, Wade pulled her fingers out of me. She gently ran them through my wetness and then stopped, her whole hand cupping me, holding my cunt. I pulled her hand off my mouth and lay there panting as she smoothed my bangs off my forehead, kissing my cheek, my eyelids, my neck.

"How are you, sweetheart?"

I pulled her down and curled into her. She was grinning, very pleased with herself, I'm sure. As I shifted I could feel that my cum was soaking through my overalls. I groaned.

"Wade, it looks like I pissed myself! How am I going to say good-bye to the O'Connellys covered in come?"

"I don't know, sugar, but a fair amount squirted out on me, so I guess we're in the same boat."

I looked, and indeed she had a patch of wet soaking the front of her shirt. How had I ejaculated so much come without even realizing it? Still, we weren't exactly in the same boat. It didn't look like she had pissed her pants.

"I have an idea." Her eyes lit when she said it. "Come with me."

She pulled her hand out of my pants, stroking my throbbing clit once more as she did so, making me twitch, and kissed me. Standing up, she reached down to help me to my feet. My legs felt shaky and I buttoned the fly of my overalls as Wade walked to the edge of the loft and looked over. "The coast is clear," she said, grinning like crazy. "Let's go."

My eyes narrowed in suspicion. Whatever was making her smile like that, my intuition advised caution. But I followed her down the ladder and stood in one dark corner of the barn, waiting to see what madness she was up to. I was looking closely at the antique scythes hanging on the wall when I heard her turn on the hose and felt the frigid water hit me full blast.

"AHHHHH!!!! WADE! I HATE you!" My lungs seized up in shock at the cold and I gasped for breath. Turning around, I pushed her away hard, but not before she got the hose down the front of my overalls. "OHHH, YOU!!!" I got control of the hose and turned it on her, hitting her right in the face. She put up her hands, sputtering, and called surrender.

"OKAY! OKAY! STOP!"

I knew I had wanted a shower, but this was ridiculous. I

turned off the hose, still furious, while she doubled over in hysterical laughter. Later I would admit that it was a good plan, but that didn't make me any less pissed, or my sensitive pussy any less cold. I threw the hose down, about to advance upon her, when I looked up to see half our work crew and Mr. O'Connelly staring at us with open mouths. Well...later. Wade was going to get it.

So I said good-bye to my employers soaking from head to toe with indistinguishable wetness. All in all, it wasn't that bad a way to end a job.

VIENNA

Kell Brannon

Stefan, standing behind me in the stranger's apartment, eases my coat off of my shoulders. The reality of this situation finally dawns on me and I realize that I am on display, here in this strange room, this strange city. Stefan's city. My heart thuds in my chest and I struggle to make myself breathe evenly, in, out, in.

The man is beautiful, I'll admit, and I gaze at his pale eyes and the sharp bones of his face, a contrast to Stefan's dark, intense features. Stefan has been my only company for weeks now, and it startles me to be confronted so closely with another person, to meet friendly eyes. The man smiles just a little, as if to reassure me, and examines my body without embarrassment.

Stefan speaks, in German, and of course

I cannot understand it; the man responds in a measured cadence, his voice low. The smile and the ease in his squared shoulders tell me that he is pleased, and that nothing about our late visit comes as a surprise.

Clearly Stefan knows the man, but he has never spoken of him. Whether he is a colleague or an old friend, or perhaps even a new one, I have no idea.

Tonight Stefan asked me to dress only in the simple black bra and panties he admires, and to wear my long coat and boots, protection from the cold.

"And wear your hair down and loose," he said. "For me."

I thought this would simply be another of Stefan's games. I thought he would take me to a performance, or maybe a movie, and ask me to open my coat for him when the lights went down.

Of course. For you.

But I was unprepared for this.

His hand slides up my spine and into my hair. He takes a fistful, close to the base of my skull, and pulls my head back just a little. He knows what this does to me now, and he plays me like a violin. The response between my legs is almost Pavlovian, and I am instantly wet, despite the stranger standing just a few feet away, watching such an intense and vulnerable moment. I would never tell friends about the effect Stefan has on me, or about the things I let him do.

"Lena?" he whispers. The stranger has me locked in his gaze, and I see such confidence there, such expectation, that I am transfixed. Stefan gives my hair another sharp tug. "Answer."

"Y-Yes, Stefan."

"I want you to use your mouth on this man. Like I taught you."

I have never done such a thing, never been shared—but I am dazed by the heady anticipation between the two men, and by the attention they focus on me.

"You want me to…? But you didn't—"

"Yes. To begin."

I feel the pit of my stomach turn to ice and fall away inside me.

"Stefan, what is this? Why didn't you tell me first?"

"Because I did not want to tell you." The stranger calmly observes us, obviously in no rush. Stefan leans in, whispers more quietly: "Lena, if this is too much, ever, say our word."

Our word? Our word. I dredge it from memory. Over dinner, once, he laughingly asked me for a special word, a secret one that I would only use when I truly wanted him to stop.

At the time, it didn't dawn on me that the question was preparation for a test. For a series of tests. I had almost forgotten it, preferring instead to sink into this experiment of submission, the feeling that I might belong to him entirely, if only for a little while.

But now the word shines in my mind, glows at the back of my tongue.

"I remember."

I survey the stranger as he takes a step closer to us. He is not as tall or as stocky as Stefan, but he is well built. My mind flashes back to a night when Stefan exhausted me completely, yet kept going, licking me to another excruciating peak when he knew I was too feeble to pull him back into my arms. I feel Stefan's chest rise and fall as he slowly releases his grip on my hair. He speaks to the man again, and then murmurs into my ear: "Do it. For me."

The man takes another step, close enough now for me to kiss; I consider doing so, but tears prick my eyes, and I can't go through with it. The intimacy of tasting those thin, smooth lips, after these strange, isolated weeks with Stefan, might shatter me.

Stefan's hands press my shoulders, and I drop to my knees as I feel him move away. The stranger's eyes never leave mine. He undoes his belt, then the button at his jeans.

As if possessed, my hand drifts to the zipper and pulls it down, revealing that the man is wearing nothing under the jeans. I nearly laugh aloud; how quaint, how like a movie, that we are both so prepared!

The jeans slide over his slender hips, then down; he presses closer, enough so that I can smell the sweet remnant of a shower on his skin. The cock is of average size, well shaped with a slight bend to one side, not quite erect. I trace the man's hip with one thumb, along the bone and into the crease where his leg meets the fur at his pubis, and lick my lips. Stefan watches me intently from a comfortable chair a few feet away.

The man waits. We all wait, the moment lengthening between us like a shadow. I look up again at the stranger, and I slowly touch my wet lips to his glans, listen to his breath catch in his throat.

Perhaps it was foolish of me to return to Vienna with Stefan, simply to keep his company for so many weeks.

We are still new to each other, so new that we still go for days without having a real conversation. The bond is sustained by our sweat and the sounds of our flesh meeting. When we have our morning meal or share the mirror over the tiny sink in our rented room, we fall into awkward, sheepish silence.

There is not yet a reservoir of small talk we can dip into, no shared books, events, politics.

But we are in no hurry. We are buoyed along by lust, by our inexplicable hunger to be together.

And, of course, there are the games.

During the day, I am not yet brave enough to venture out alone, so I wear his oversized button-down shirts and sip cheap tea, gazing out at pedestrians and birds and architecture. In secret I fancy myself a kept woman, a pet, which I would never tolerate back in the States.

At evenings, he returns to our room, and there is deep hunger in his eyes. I can sense him holding it back while he inquires about my comfort. I am ever touched by his concern that I am happy, alone and utterly dependent in this foreign city, his home.

Sometimes it is enough to make love—no, let us be honest; we fuck—as the fading light streams in and bathes the dusty walls in yellow light.

Sometimes he needs more from me than this. On these nights he explores me relentlessly, to see how far I will go to indulge him. He fondles me in taxicabs; he runs his hand up my skirt, under tables and against buildings. He makes me stand in the middle of our rented room and tells me to pleasure myself. He bought me a false cock for this purpose. The awkward stance the act required was hard to maintain and distracted me from the pleasure. I kept it going anyway, even after I was sore, because I loved seeing his hand on his own cock, his eyes glazed as he stared at my dripping cunt.

One evening, not long ago, he tied a silk scarf over my eyes; he led me to the center of the room and bound me, bent over a chair, spread wide. Once I was secure in the bonds, he slowed in his other ministrations, as if preparing for a ritual. He caressed me tenderly and slowly, pressed his thumb into my mouth to suck, kissed the fleshy swells at the sides of my breasts where they were pressed outward by the seat.

This was entirely new to me, and I was frightened by it; I was made quite uncomfortable by the ropes, the awkward height of the seat, the burn on my knees from the carpet. I was so wet that I could feel beads of my moisture escape and soak my pubic hair. Throughout this ordeal he left the blindfold on, and he never touched me between the legs, though I begged until I was hoarse. The din of the street coming in through our open window obscured the sound of his breath.

When he finally knelt behind me, he drove into me deep and steadily, with no prelude. He wrapped one fist in my hair, tugged my head back.

This brought discoveries for both of us.

What I discovered is that the greed and fear inspired in this kind of sex, at least between Stefan and me, is as intoxicating as the fucking itself. My modern sensibilities tell me that I should feel degraded, humiliated. Instead I feel relieved, free of the need to make even small decisions.

I discovered great joy in having my body used. He may have understood this before I did.

What he discovered was this: If he takes me hard from behind under the right circumstances, with a rhythm that is relentless and can be trusted to keep up as long as I want it, I can come so hard that I faint. And that if he keeps fucking, I might wake up and come again.

The stranger's scrotum presses my chin as I work the head of his penis with my throat, fluttering the muscles around it.

When I steal a glance upward I see that his head is thrown back and his eyes are closed. He and Stefan have been murmuring to each other, and Stefan has given me a few words of instruction, in a low, even voice. Whether the requests came from the man or from Stefan himself, I do not know.

The latest words: "No hands, Lena."

Stefan prefers that my hands never touch his cock while I please him orally.

I hold on to the man's thigh with one hand, dropping the other into my lap, with every intention of addressing the slow throb that builds there.

"Take his balls."

I suck lightly as I let the cock slide from my throat, press it with my tongue while it glides past my lips and out of my mouth, springing upward with a tiny, wet pop. The man flinches, breathing heavily. I drift lower and slurp at a testicle, mouthing it tenderly, drawing one soft egg between my lips, then the other, as Stefan loves me to do for him. The stranger loves it as well; I feel him part his legs and press closer to give me better access.

"The hand, Lena."

I pull my hand away from my lap, but it is too late. My lover has left the chair, and now he kneels close behind me, pulling both of my arms back and away. He holds my wrists loosely together with one of his own big hands, against his thighs. With his other hand he reaches around to fondle my breast, then traces the outline of my cheek and jaw. He traces along the corner of my lip, and I imagine his fingertip brushing against the stranger's skin where it enters my mouth. I wonder if they have shared a woman in this manner before.

The stranger moans, murmurs to Stefan.

He then pulls his testes out of my mouth, angles his cock down, presses it gently into my mouth again. I greedily comply, any hesitation long gone, and I swallow him immediately, pulling him in as deeply as our contours will allow. He is far along now; I feel him instinctively begin to thrust, sliding into and out of my throat, and I want so badly to excite him further with my hand. Stefan's fingers tenderly trace the soft underside of my jaw and throat, feeling the geographies change. I shift so that I can move my hands a little within Stefan's constraint; I clumsily trace my way up his thighs until I find his cock. He sighs, swelling into the curl of my fingers.

The stranger buries his hands in my hair to guide my motion, back and forth. My cunt clenches in the same rhythm, aching to be filled, to be taken by both of them in turn. My mouth makes the wet, sucking sounds that used to embarrass me when I fellate Stefan in our empty room; they excite me now.

The stranger cries out, quietly, and pulls himself from my mouth. I hadn't realized that my eyes were closed; I open them now, panting and confused, and see that Stefan's hand is massaging the stranger's testes, rolling them gently against his body with his palm.

I almost come, then and there, just from the sight of this.

"Yes," he breathes, into my neck. "Watch me."

Stefan moves on to take the wet cock into his hand, giving it the same firm, steady rhythm I tried so hard to create with my mouth, just as he'd taught me. I drift out of myself, rise above the scene, and watch Stefan's strong, square hand stroking the cock, pointing the head of it toward my chest. I see myself waiting for the inevitable spurt of heat along my skin, gazing at the hand and the cock and the sheen of my own saliva.

Stefan whispers into my ear. "Do you trust me?"

I lean back into his chest, trembling. I thought I knew this man, and I thought I knew who I was in his presence; but there are depths to him that I cannot fathom. All I know is that I need him. I feel more alive right now, and more awake, than I have in years.

"Yes."

"I will never hurt you, Lena. Not really."

"I know."

The stranger groans again, a deep, guttural sound, and I feel the change in atmosphere as his body tenses further. Behind me, as the moment approaches, Stefan's cock lurches in the awkward grip of my fingers.

WET

Donna George Storey

I'll be honest. I like my sex a little rough. And very wet. Sure, I started out like most women, wanting valentines and sweet words, but all along I was waiting for the right moment, that perfect slap on the ass, to teach me what I really needed. For me, enlightenment came the year after college, when I taught English in Japan—a country that understands pleasure is always sweeter when it comes with a little suffering.

My first months in Kyoto brought hardship aplenty. I'd found myself a one-room apartment above a rice shop in a farming village west of the city. At about forty bucks a month, the rent was right, but the room was so cold I could see my breath when I woke up in the morning. Then I had to stumble outside to the

toilet, a squat-style affair located by the stairwell. A bath required a ten-minute walk through the rice paddies to the *sentô*.
A long soak in the huge tub was pure luxury, but first I had
to endure the gaze of the creepy attendant who watched me
undress from his pulpitlike platform with shameless curiosity.
Sometimes I wonder how I put up with it all, but at twenty-
two I was a romantic and more than ready to renounce the
comforts of my wall-to-wall-carpet childhood for the sake of
intercultural understanding. Indeed, each hardship gave me a
voluptuous thrill, as if I were sinking deeper into the embrace
of a stern and exacting lover.

But the public bath had its pleasures, too. Beyond the frigid
dressing room lay a tropical paradise of gleaming white tile. A
semicircular tub the size of a small hotel pool filled the entire
left half of the bathing room. To the right was a row of fau-
cets, where a line of nude women knelt as if in worship, legs
tucked beneath them, their heart-shaped asses resting on their
feet, Japanese-style. Sometimes I couldn't help imagining how
jealous my male friends back home would be. Wasn't it every
hot guy's fantasy to be surrounded by naked women caressing
their own bodies with soapy-slick hands, eyes closed and lips
parted in pleasure?

I wasn't supposed to have such thoughts in this temple
of bodily purification. Bathing was obviously serious business in Japan. I quickly got the basics down, but as I took
my place at an empty faucet each night, I still cast sideways
glances at my companions for tips on the proper technique.
I noticed that they always sloshed a basinful of hot water over
their backs and chests, and then went to work with the soap
and washcloth, scrubbing each inch of skin with almost religious zeal. Although I tried my best to polish each knee for

what seemed like an hour, I could never outlast them.

What filthy things had these prim ladies done to get their bodies so dirty?

This was only one of the forbidden thoughts that swirled through my brain as I sank into the soaking tub at last, my muscles melting to caramel in the steaming water. More distracting still were the sounds drifting over the partition from the men's side of the bath. I tried to keep my thoughts clean, but with all the splashes and sighs and deep male voices gliding through the mist, it was pretty hopeless.

Of course I knew most of those low, sexy voices belonged to farmers I'd seen working in the rice paddies, their faces wizened and brown from decades of hard labor. They were hardly fodder for sexual fantasy. Still at least one or two of the guys had to be acceptably young and attractive. Maybe it was the gorgeous college boy I spotted on the train platform each morning? Or the young office worker with the velvety eyes who kept glancing shyly in my direction at the convenience store?

Before long I was dizzy from the heat, the steam, the X-rated images flickering in my head. I closed my eyes and felt the pulsing water caress my flesh like a warm hand, felt my other lips, down there, plump and ready for him, my lover, so handsome and willing to do every dirty thing I could imagine. Those hungry lips would call to him, silently, through the moist, dripping air.

Come. Teach me. Please.

He rises from the tub, the water falling from his sculpted torso like a veil, and crosses over to the women's side of the bath, heedless of the attendant's jealous scowl. Intent on his goal, he slides the door open and strides right in, although he does hold his towel discreetly over his cock in deference to the other ladies. They titter and hurry to cover themselves with their hands, but he doesn't even glance their way.

He's come only for me.

"Get out of the bath," he orders in gruff Japanese. "You're still dirty. Obviously you need a lesson on how to wash properly."

Heart pounding, I climb out of the water and kneel at the closest faucet, my head bowed.

I know I am a very dirty girl, indeed.

The teacher snaps my washcloth open like a whip and soaps it to a lather. The first part of the curriculum involves scrubbing my back vigorously from my shoulders to my buttocks. Each stroke finds an answering twinge in my belly. My pale skin is already flushed from the hot bath, but under his scouring, my flesh blushes to a fiery hue. I am red and wet down there, too, because I can feel my own pussy juice oozing onto my legs. When the teacher reaches my hips, he lays the cloth aside and gives my ass a good kneading with his bare hands, then finishes with a stinging slap, one for each cheek.

The spanking shoots up my spine like an electric shock. I can't restrain a low moan, pain mixed with desire.

"I see you're enjoying the lesson," he observes coolly, "but you have much study ahead. I'm going to wash the front of you now, but first you must sit up like a proper Japanese lady. Come now, shoulders back, chin up."

Obediently I square my hunched shoulders, but keep my arms crossed modestly over my chest. Clicking his tongue, the teacher reaches around and grabs my wrists, pulling them apart to reveal my breasts, shimmering with a film of moisture, the nipples pink and erect.

"Let me clean you," he murmurs. "Let me show you how to do it right."

He cups my breasts in his soapy hands and rubs me, circling round and round as if he's polishing two plump apples. My nipples, it seems, are especially filthy for he rolls them between his fingers for the longest time, pinching and tweaking until I'm nearly sobbing with lust. Through half-veiled eyes, I notice the women have gathered around us, their eyes glued to the obscene show. Some even caress their own breasts, mimicking the teacher's movements.

"Now I want you to lie back and spread your legs. I know you need a very good scrubbing down there."

What else can I do but obey? Though I've always been a good student, always gone for that *A,* I have to admit my desire to please the teacher has never been this strong.

Easing back onto the cool tile, I inch my legs open.

Look how pink and swollen it is! It's as juicy as a ripe peach! She is dirty, just like the teacher said....

A chorus of female voices echoes through the steam. Flustered and ashamed, I snap my legs closed.

"No chatter during class time, ladies," the teacher warns sternly. "You there and you, make yourself useful. Hold her legs open so we can continue with our study."

Two pairs of soft hands force my knees open and press them to the floor.

"Would you like the washcloth now, Sensei?" the woman at my right leg asks respectfully.

"No," the teacher replies, "there are too many delicate folds down there for a cloth to get clean. For this part of the lesson, I must use my tongue."

He bends over and gives my swollen slit one lingering lick, like a cat, followed by delicate, probing flicks as he seeks my sweet spot. The way I arch and whimper tells him that he's found it. He cleans me there—the strokes quickening to a lashing—until I groan and thrash against the hands of my captors. I'm just about to come when he pulls away. "Time to rinse."

Before I can protest that perhaps the Honorable Teacher might consider cleaning me like that just a little longer, my exposed pussy is flooded with a basinful of hot water. Tendrils of flame shoot through my belly and I squirm, my body sloshing about on the slick floor.

The teacher seems pleased with my progress, but we have one final lesson.

"It's time to clean you inside now." Grinning, he begins to soap up his cock, his member grower longer and fatter with every stroke. In the end he is huge, as thick as a young tree trunk, plump purple veins throbbing through the flesh. It's a dick straight out of a floating world print.

"I don't think I can take that thing inside me," I plead, staring at his cock with undisguised horror.

"Even if something is hard," he intones wisely, "you can succeed if you want it very much and you try your best."

I breathe deeply, preparing myself for the ordeal to come. I do want this—very much.

He nods to his assistants who lock their hands under my ass and tilt my hips up to meet him. Nudging my hole gently with the head of his cock, he pushes in with aching slowness.

I can feel him all the way up through my chest, my neck, and my skull. I've never felt so stretched, so full. My teacher begins to move, swiveling his hips to scour and polish every inch of my insides with his rigid tool. Feminine murmurs of approval and envy rise up around me. I open my eyes to see the other women kneeling closer, their eyes fixed on the place where his cock enters my body. I see, too, that they are masturbating as they watch us. The shy ones rub their washcloths between their legs tentatively, as if it's all just part of an ordinary bath. The bolder ones dispense with pretense, their fingers dancing shamelessly over their slits. One lady is even brazen enough to tweak her neighbor's nipple while she strums herself.

I see it all now, everything. We're all dirty. We all want to cleanse ourselves. And this is Japan, where a group effort always gets the job done best. As if they've read my thoughts, the lady on my right begins to stroke my breast; from the left comes a tongue to tease my other nipple. Lips close over mine from above, female lips, meltingly soft. Flesh envelops me everywhere, pulsing with desire, lapping, sucking, pounding into me deeper and harder, until with a cry of release, I am finally clean. And all thanks to his lesson—a little rough, very wet, and just the way l like it.

As I strolled home from the *sentô* in the moonlight, my flesh still warm and tingling, I knew the chances were slim I'd ever really find myself in the middle of an orgy in a public bath. On the other hand, it was reasonably likely that some day I'd meet an attractive young man who'd be willing to give me a hands-on lesson in Japanese bathing techniques.

In fact, my wish did come true in a peculiarly Japanese way—through an introduction by a go-between, like the marriage meetings of old. Early in the new year, I started a teaching job at a pharmaceutical factory in Shiga. The friendly in-house teacher, Sherry, immediately took me under her wing. She was already engaged to a Japanese guy she'd met in the

States and was all for setting me up with someone, too. It just so happened she knew the perfect guy, a Mr. Yamada who worked in the main office in Osaka.

Sherry ran down his vital statistics. Mr. Yamada was twenty-six, went to a good college and had his own apartment. (I imagined his bathroom, small but with a luxurious cedar tub and a traditional lantern in the corner, glowing softly.) He was good looking and stockier than most Japanese. (A nice broad saddle would be a plus when I got on top and rode him to a lather.) His English was pretty good. (Not a minus, but how much talking would we do anyway?) And he'd traveled to Europe on his own, not in a tour group. (This showed a hunger for adventure that would surely translate well into wild moves on a slippery bathroom floor.)

"How soon can we meet?" I asked her without missing a beat.

That's how I found myself in a fancy café, gazing into the eyes of the fetching Mr. Yamada and wondering how many more formalities we had to endure until we could get naked and rub our soapy bodies together. Mr. Yamada was apparently more patient than I was, but he seemed to have similar ideas because three dates later, he invited me to his place.

The first thing I asked for was a tour—an American custom, I explained. His apartment was very different from mine, with all the modern comforts. An electric heater purred softly in the corner, chasing back the February chill. The dining-kitchen had a Western-style table and chairs; the bedroom was equipped with a bed and dresser. Even the traditional *tatami* straw-matted living room was transformed into a high-tech wonderland by an elaborate entertainment system spread out along three walls.

"Would it be too rude if I asked to see your bath? They're so different from what we have in America."

"Of course," he said in his careful English, slightly baffled by the request, but eager to accommodate the foreign guest's wishes.

He led me over to a door next to the bedroom and pushed it open.

My heart sank.

I was expecting it to be small, but I hadn't imagined something this distressingly modern: an all-in-one cubicle fashioned from a seamless expanse of beige plastic. The toilet, sink and shower bath were crammed together so tightly that if we tried to play out my bathing teacher fantasy, we'd be knocking our heads against the john.

"Thanks, it's very nice." I stepped back, forcing my lips into a smile.

Mr. Yamada sensed he'd disappointed me. "Shall we drink coffee? I bought apple pie at the bakery. I hear Americans like such things."

I nodded, blushing at my own selfishness. The kind invitation to his home was my chance to learn more about him as a person, not lure him into some kinky sex game I'd dreamed up to get myself off on lonely nights in my futon. I silently vowed to be the perfect guest for the rest of the visit, pure in thought and deed.

I was doing a fairly good job of it as we lounged on floor pillows on the *tatami* listening to jazz and snacking on apple tart. But then Mr. Yamada put down his coffee cup, gazed into my eyes, and leaned over to kiss me.

At first all he did was kiss me, for the longest time, as if some secret rule of etiquette dictated a good host could go no further on the first visit. Yet the languid dance of our tongues was having a surprisingly powerful effect on my body, rather like a soaking in a hot bath. Soon every muscle was so soft and rubbery that I collapsed onto the pillow, pulling him down with me.

Now he did use his hands, gently stroking my cheek, my neck, my breasts, and especially my nipples poking up stiffly through my sweater. The fluid warmth, the exquisite care in his touch got me so turned on, my panties were drenched. I feared I'd be leaving quite a wet spot on his pristine straw mat.

"I want you," I whispered.

He smiled and pulled a box of tissues and a condom from the nearby bookshelf—how courteous of him to anticipate his guest's needs before the fact—then undressed us both quickly. He lay back and I straddled him. I was ready to slide right on, but to my surprise he grabbed my hips and pulled me forward so my dripping pussy rested on his taut belly. Instinctively I rocked into him, coating him with my juices. Our bodies made soft sucking sounds as I glided over him, almost as if we were all soaped together in a steamy *sentô*.

Mr. Yamada seemed perfectly content to let me massage him with my drooling pussy all afternoon. I was the one who finally lost patience. Rising up on my knees, I shifted backward, impaling myself on his cock. The seawater smell of female arousal mingled with the sweet, grassy fragrance of *tatami* straw. I realized, with a delicious twinge of guilt, that I'd been a very bad girl this afternoon. Because I hadn't really given up my selfish fantasy at all. I was reaching out for it, hungrily, in all its liquid pleasure. Hotter and wetter than I'd even imagined, it was almost in my grasp.

By cherry blossom time I was spending every weekend at Mr. Yamada's apartment—I was calling him Shinji now—and the sex just kept getting wetter and better. We hadn't yet taken a real bath together, but I did confess that I liked going to the *sentô*. My fondness for old-fashioned Japanese things always amused him. He laughed and told me that his grandmother still went to the public bath, but young people only did that on vacation at a hot spring in the mountains or an inn by the sea.

"Is that so?" I replied with an innocent smile.

Naturally, from that moment on, my mind was busy spinning out a naughty scheme. Shinji was so sweet about going along with my every whim; I knew he'd easily agree to a weekend at a mountain spa with a rustic coed bath. But I wasn't so sure about the rough stuff I secretly craved—the gruff orders, the spanking, the sweet humiliations. On the other hand, Japanese men were historically known for their lordly, selfish ways and a rather domineering treatment of the fair sex. Perhaps taking Shinji to a traditional mountain inn would allow him to tap into his inner samurai?

I figured it wouldn't hurt to do what I could to nudge him in that direction.

After all, the hot spring was almost a national institution of sensual indulgence. For hardworking Japanese, it provided the perfect chance to shrug off the rules of ordinary life by dining on elaborate gourmet meals in their bathrobes, taking endless baths and, ideally, fucking as much as possible. As soon as we got to the inn, Shinji did suddenly seem more intent on hedonistic pleasure. After our nine-course dinner of fish stew, Kobe beef dripping with butter, and fluffy white rice served with jewel-colored pickles, he claimed he was still hungry. He proceeded to push me back on the futon, spread my thighs and feast on my pussy. When he had me so hot I was begging for it, he flipped me over and took me from behind, slamming his cock into me with uncharacteristic abandon. I came so hard, I wondered if I'd be physically capable of getting off again down in the bath, which of course was the intended climax of the trip from the start.

I hadn't told Shinji the details of my plan yet. I merely suggested, with a twinkle in my eye, that we go for one last soak together before we went to sleep.

The grand bath was deserted when we arrived, just as I had hoped, although in theory, a few willing lesbians would have made for the perfect translation of my fantasy. Still, I couldn't have ordered a more beautiful scene. The water was as smooth as glass; wisps of steam hovered like specters in the golden light of the lanterns glowing in each corner of the room.

Shinji shrugged off his cotton robe and went to the faucet to wash off the lingering stickiness of our lovemaking.

Smiling devilishly, I headed straight for the tub.

"Aren't you going to wash first?" he called after me.

I turned and gave him a bratty smirk. "What if I don't want to?"

"You must." He usually laughed at my lapses of etiquette, but this taboo was too strong for the usual indulgence.

I held my foot over the water as if I were about to step in. "I guess I am pretty dirty after what we did tonight, but I'm just not in the mood to do it."

He frowned. For the first time, I think he was truly angry with me.

"In Japan, you must wash before you get in the bath. It is the proper way."

"Oh, yeah? Well maybe you'll just have to teach me how to do it right."

His frown deepened. I met his gaze defiantly. Then I smiled.

His eyes flickered. I think that's when he finally got it, because in two long strides he was at my side, grabbing my arm and hauling me back to the faucet. With a downward tug, he forced me to my knees. He quickly filled the wooden basin with steaming water and splashed it over my chest and shoulders. I cried out softly. Kneeling behind me, he wrapped his arms around me, but it was more a punishment than an embrace.

I don't think I'd ever been so turned on in my life.

"I will wash you now," he whispered.

"Yes. Teach me how. I'm dirty," I confessed in a low voice. "My breasts, they're very dirty. Maybe you have to scrub hard."

"Is that so?" There was no doubt now he'd caught on to the game. "Why are they so dirty?"

"I let a man kiss them and suck them."

"Yes, then I think you are very dirty." He took the bar of soap and began to rub the flat side over my nipples. Pinpricks of pleasure shot straight to my pussy. A beguiling combination of smooth and hard, it was even better than my fantasy.

"What about between your legs?" he murmured.

"Yes. It's very dirty. I let a man...take me...from behind."

"That is dirty. Like an animal. I must clean you there very well." He picked up the washcloth, draped it over his fingers and pressed it between my pussy lips. His movements were subtle—firm, slow circles over my clit—but the flesh there was already swollen and sore from the earlier fucking. I had to grit my teeth to bear it, but I also found myself pushing into his hand with small rocking motions to intensify the sensation.

"Spread your legs a little. Now we will rinse." He took a

basin of steaming water and splashed it vigorously over my slit. It streamed down my thighs, mingling with my juices. My cunt was on fire, my skin a throbbing scarlet hue. When I imagined how it would go, I was hoping this part would last an hour, but now I wanted him inside me so badly I was shaking.

"Shinji? Can we do it here? Now?"

He took me in his arms again, more tenderly, his erection pressing against the cleft of my ass. "I'm sorry. I don't have a condom."

I groaned in disappointment, but I could hardly blame him for the oversight. Still, my primitive life in the countryside had taught me I could adapt to inconvenience when I had to. "Can we go back to the room?"

He paused.

I held my breath.

"No," he barked, in a very passable impression of an imperious samurai lord.

My heart skipped a beat. It wasn't the answer I wanted. And it was.

"I am not finished washing you. This place for example. It is still very dirty." He ran his fingertip between my buttocks to tap the tight ring of my asshole, a caress that sizzled straight to my toes, my teeth, the backs of my eyeballs. This had never been part of my fantasy either—but it would be now.

"No. Stop." In my shame and surprise, the word escaped my lips before I really knew what I was saying.

"No? You don't want this?" he asked, his voice suddenly soft.

The finger pulled away.

My chest was churning with confusion, desire, regret. What

did I really want? For so long I thought it was a good, hard fucking on a wet bathroom floor, but I knew now the longing went deeper. What I really wanted was for Shinji to force me to do...exactly what I wanted. Which didn't really make sense. Except here, in the humid warmth of the bath, it suddenly did.

"I do want it, Shinji. Please, clean me there."

I sighed as the finger returned, stroking and teasing my newfound pleasure button. This was exactly what I wanted. Lips grazed my neck, gliding softly over the wet skin, a tender surprise. I discovered I wanted that, too. And then—smack—another surprise, a sharp slap on my vulva, aimed just so to send waves of heat through my tingling clit.

How could it possibly get better than this?

"Yes, oh god, yes," I moaned, jerking my hips forward to show him I was ready for more.

Shinji made a strange sound, low in his throat. The spanking quickened. On the verge of climax, a weird image flashed into my head: a woman's nude body, poised on tiptoe at the edge of a tub, one trembling foot stretching higher and farther, until she tipped over into the deep water. And then I was falling, too, a soft howl rising from my throat as I came. The spanking stopped, and Shinji held me tight in one arm, while his other hand diddled my asshole until my deepest shudders subsided.

I expected an embrace, the customary conclusion to our lovemaking, but tonight Shinji had other ideas. Without a word, he pushed me facedown on the wet floor and straddled my thighs. Moments later, my ass and back were showered with a spray of hot, pulsing liquid. It wasn't from a basin, that much was certain.

I hadn't planned on an ending like this, with me facedown

on a bathroom floor, drenched with the spunk of my lover, who knelt over me, his dripping cock in his hand. But as with a translation, the exact expression was less important than the meaning. This was my dream come true, a scene as wet and dirty as I could ask for.

But, to be honest, I had never felt so clean.

PLEASE

Xan West

I met him on a Wednesday night at this bar on
the Lower East Side. I don't usually go to bars,
but I wanted to shoot some nine-ball and get
out some of the nervous aggressive energy that
had been riding me all day. I put my name up
in chalk and he caught my eye. I admit I especially enjoyed watching him bend over the
table. There was something bad about him.
It wasn't the ink, or the chain on his wallet;
almost everyone in the bar had those. It was
his eyes. The same eyes as that leopard in the
Bronx Zoo. I can sit on a bench and just watch
that leopard for hours, mesmerized by its feral
grace. His eyes captured me just like that.

I admit I bent over a bit more than I usually
would when it was my turn to play him. I know
it's an obvious thing to do. But I couldn't help

it. There's something luscious about bending over in just the right way in the pants I was wearing. The cotton is worn and soft, and it caresses my thighs like a lover. I can never wear anything between them and my body. I found myself wondering if he could tell that just from looking. Because he definitely was looking.

We played silently. He stalked me around the table. I could feel the fear grow, and I'm generally a very confident player. I could not stop staring at him. Everything fascinated, from the taut muscles of his thighs to the thick leather band around his left wrist, to his tall black boots. I got lost looking at him.

My eyes lifted from the bulge in his jeans and I found myself staring at the table, stuck in a fantasy. I was bent over the table. His friends helped to hold me down as he smacked my ass with the pool cue. He slowly cut off my pants with his blade, teasing me with it. His boots kicked my feet apart and spread me wide. He fucked me right there: my wrists clamped down by his friends, a pool ball stuck in my mouth to muffle my screams, as he pounded his cock into me.

I was lost in the imagined feel of him fucking me, my cunt throbbing. He had to clear his throat a few times.

"It's your turn," he said.

I tried for a carom off the five and the nine ball missed the pocket. I handed him the cue, and our hands brushed. I met his eyes and momentarily stopped breathing. He just held my gaze, smiling.

"I'm Christian," he said.

"I'm Jewish," I mumbled.

He chuckled, and it was a low delicious sound.

"No," he said. "My name is Christian."

He reached out, and his thumb stroked my hand, waiting.

My mouth was dry. I couldn't speak. I cleared my throat.

"I'm Jamie."

"Hello there, Jamie," he said, his hand still gripping mine. I swallowed, trying to figure out what to say. Then he released me. He chalked up his cue, his eyes looking me up and down. He made that shot. Just rammed that nine ball home with the five, and the game was over. He walked over to me, getting a bit too close, his eyes on the rapid pulse in my throat. He rubbed his thumb over that spot and then lifted his hand to show me the smudge of blue chalk he had removed.

"Want to play?" His voice was raspy with teasing invitation.

"Play? We just did," I said.

"How 'bout a different sort of game?"

He raised one eyebrow and smiled. I didn't know what to say. Could he mean what I was thinking?

"Want me to show you?"

"Please," I said, hoping.

He took my hand and led me around the corner, tossing his cue on the table as we left. He took me into a large single-stall bathroom and locked the door. He stepped away from the door, freeing my path to run, if I wanted to.

"Here are the rules. I do what I want to you. You don't touch me without permission. If you want me to stop, you say 'stop.' That is the only word that will stop me, but if I hear it, I will stop immediately. I won't do anything that could harm you, but I may want to hurt you a little, and I definitely want to fuck you. Are you game?"

My eyes felt like they were going to pop out of my head. I just stood there, looking at him. I had played this kind of game before, but never with a stranger. The reckless feeling that had been riding me all day filled my throat, pushing me. I was damn tempted. I had never wanted anything as much as I wanted to be in his power in that moment.

"Please," I said softly.

And then his hands were on me. He gripped my wrists, holding them tight behind my back, and started licking my exposed skin. I tilted my head back, offering him my neck. His cock was pressing into my thigh and I could feel my cunt contract in response to its closeness. His hand stroked my throat, and his thigh thrust between mine, backing me up against the sink. My heart started to pound. I was really doing this.

He turned me over, yanked down my pants, and just stopped, staring at my naked ass. He chuckled, a smooth gravelly sound.

"Oh, you are my kind of girl," he said.

I started trembling. I wanted him inside me. He bent me over the sink, unzipped his fly, slid on a condom, and then he was there, deep inside, in one quick thrust. The porcelain was cold against my nipples, and I was shakily gripping the sink, trying to stay balanced, but all I could feel was his cock. It was the hardest, thickest cock I had ever been fucked with. I was biting my lip trying to keep quiet, and it was a losing battle.

I felt so full, and he just kept driving into me. The invasion was intense. Every time my cunt contracted it felt like it was too much, like I couldn't take it—I was stuffed too full of him. I started holding my breath to keep from screaming. The pounding in my cunt matched the pounding in my head until I felt like I was going to pass out. His hand was in my hair, pulling my head back, and I could feel his breath on my neck as he spoke to me.

"Breathe, dammit."

I did. I breathed in and I felt my pelvis tilt just a bit, and then he was slamming into my cervix. His hand was still gripping my hair as he kept hitting my cervix just right and I knew I was going to come. I took my own fist into my mouth and I bit down to keep from screaming as I spasmed around his massive girth. He was still there, still so hard inside me. His hand still twisted in my hair, pulling it in these rhythmic pulses that felt just like sex. It was too much. I couldn't take it. I started to beg.

"Please. Please. Please."

"Please what, girl? What do you want?"

I went silent. Then I was whimpering as he continued to fuck me, and it felt so good and was too much all at once. He was so hard and I wanted him to stop and I wanted him never to stop.

"Please," I whispered.

"You know what to say if you want me to stop. Is that what you want?"

He went still inside me. I was throbbing around him and I started grinding into the sink. My clit was pulsing and I had no idea what I had wanted a moment before, but I knew what I wanted right then.

"Please don't stop fucking me," I begged, before I could lose the words.

He didn't stop. The words opened a dam inside me and as he was fucking me I couldn't stop begging. He started ramming me harder, pulling my hips toward him, spreading my legs. His cock was running over that delicious spot inside me and it was amazing. The words spilled from my lips.

"Oh god, yes. Please. Please. Please. Yes. Please don't stop. Please fuck me."

He started teasing my nipples with his fingertips. They were so hard and cold that even that light silky touch hurt. Then he was twisting them and the pain was electric and sharp. It felt so good, mixing up with the relentless fucking into this long glorious spasm. He started pinching them harder and I couldn't help it, I had to slam my hips back to meet him it felt so good.

"Please don't stop. Please don't stop hurting me. Please don't stop fucking me. Please. Please. Please."

I started whimpering and I could feel the tears start. I was afraid he wouldn't understand but I couldn't stop them. It felt so good, and I was crying and coming in sharp painful bursts. It was too much, I was raw all over, and there he was still so insistently hard and deep inside me.

"Please. No more. Please."

"You know what to say. Do you want me to stop? You know the word. All you have to say is 'stop,' and I will."

"Yes. No. Oh god."

He was just there, deep inside my raw throbbing cunt. His hands dropped to my hips and he was holding on to me. Just horribly, relentlessly there. I started shuddering. My head lifted and I met his eyes in the mirror, tears still rolling down my face.

"I can stay hard inside you for hours," he said.

I came at those words. At that thought. At the promise of that, and the look in those leopard eyes, cruel and exacting. He held me there, on his cock, not letting me go. Spearing me. Claiming me. Invading me. Taking all of me. He would not let go unless I asked him to. I felt so safe. His cock didn't just fill up my cunt, it seemed to reach inside me and fill up empty spaces I didn't even know were there. I felt deliriously full of him, and it was enough to make me cry even more, my eyes spilling over. I was all wrapped up in him, and I knew this was exactly where I wanted to be.

"Your tears are so beautiful. You are incredibly sexy when you cry." His eyes held mine in the mirror.

I couldn't take that in. I just stared at him, awed, my cunt throbbing around his cock.

"Would you like it if I made you cry some more? Would you like it if I licked the tears from your cheeks? Would you like to show me how beautiful your pain can be?"

I swallowed, feeling my pupils dilating. He was suddenly scary, this man who was inside my cunt. He knew what I wanted in ways I couldn't even accept. He saw deep inside to desires I had not named for myself. I wasn't sure I was ready to be that naked. His hand reached around my body, slid between the sink and my cunt, and he moved me back a bit to accomodate it. And then he was stroking my clit, and I couldn't feel anything else. I couldn't think. It was amazing. It was shattering. I could not hold back the sounds.

"I want to hurt you. Will you like it? You know what to say if you don't want me to. You know how to stop me. Can you let yourself enjoy it? Will it make you come?"

His voice was low and soft and just as insistent as his thumb on my clit. Then I felt it. His teeth. Driving into my shoulder. Grinding into my flesh. Searing pain washed into me and I screamed. He just kept biting down harder. Sharp excruciating pain gripped my shoulder. It did not relent. It kept slamming into me, twisting around the piercing pleasure of his thumb stroking my clit. I came so hard.

Afterward, I couldn't stop trembling. He just held me as I trembled on his cock. His hand cupped my cunt, just holding me. His teeth eased off and he rested his mouth softly on my shoulder and held me as I stayed there shaking. I gazed into the mirror, certain my shoulder would be bleeding. It wasn't.

He slid out of me and tucked himself back in his pants. I turned to look at him, the tears streaming down my face. I could tell he was still rock hard, as he pulled me close, stroking the nape of my neck, murmuring in my ear.

"Your pain is gorgeous. Thank you for trusting me."

He gently licked the tears from my cheeks, smiling into my eyes. His hand stroked my cheek softly, his eyes tender.

"Please," I said.

He raised his brow. "Yes?"

I knelt on the cold tile, my eyes focused on the bulge in his jeans.

"Please?" I put everything I wanted into that one word.

He paused, caressing my hair. I looked up at him, my eyes naked. All I wanted to do was please him.

"You may," he said.

I unzipped his fly and slid out his cock. I rocked back on my heels, staring; it was still covered in a condom. It was big and red, and quite clearly silicone.

A grin slid across my face. I took it into my mouth, my eyes on his. I licked slowly up his cock, in long exaggerated strokes. I took the head into my mouth, sucking slowly. The girth was quite intense, and I needed to build up to it. I started to take him in, in slow firm strokes, building up to it. I wanted him to feel my mouth. My eyes were focused on his face, watching. I thrust my mouth onto his cock, taking him in, choking, but keeping it down. I knew he would enjoy my teary eyes. He started to groan, and his hand snaked down to tangle in my hair.

I put everything in me into sucking him. I wanted him to see how much he opened in me, how much I wanted to please him. I loved the feel of his hand guiding my head onto him. I started moving my throat in slow swallowing motions. I was aching with the size of him, but he felt so good down my throat. And then he gripped my hair and thrust into me, grunting, and I could feel his hips start to shake. I was struggling to breathe, but I knew he was coming. When he did, I came right along with him, just from the knowledge I had pleased him. He slipped out of my mouth and pulled me up to face him, smiling.

"Mmmm mmmm mmmm, you are a pleasure," he said. "How'd you like to come home with me?"

"Please," I replied.

WINTER HEAT

Saskia Walker

I look out into the drifting snow, and I think about how it stays with you—the good sex. Like echoes of the orgasm, the physical memory haunts the body. The snow today has brought with it the physical memory of the first time a man touched me, the first time a man made me come. Even now, all these years later, the memory grows tangible inside me, proving that the pleasure lasted so much longer than the moment. I sense myself growing damp as I remember every deviant thrill—every tantalizing moment and breathless discovery—as if it were yesterday.

The snow swirled around my legs as I left work that night. I was eighteen, and the icy air cut through my too-thin coat, freezing my stockings to my legs as I made my way out of the warehouse to the bus stop. My knee-high boots were coated in snow by the time I turned the corner onto the street. When I took a deep breath, the sharp cold air traveled into my lungs, quickening my senses. My heart sank when I realized I'd missed the bus.

I was stamping my feet to keep them warm when I saw a figure emerging from one of the factories further along the road. The man made a stark, dramatic outline against the white snow, smoking a cigarette as he made his way toward the bus stop. I watched him with curiosity. The way he looked attracted me instantly. He wore a leather biker's jacket—collar up against the elements—his hair pushed back over his head. Under the jacket, a white shirt and a narrow tie looked out of place on him. When he stopped alongside me, I realized I hadn't seen him around there before. He was built large but lean, his face characterized by prominent cheekbones, and wily, searching eyes. He flicked his cigarette stub into the snow and smiled when he caught my stare. I couldn't help myself. His bad-boy looks grabbed my imagination in a flash. At night, alone in my single bed in the dark, images of men like him filled my mind while I touched and stroked myself to climax. I dreamed of being taken roughly, being dirty and passionate with a man who knew how to play my body, and did it with no shame.

Watching him from under lowered eyelids, I fast forgot the cold. Forgot everything, except the lure of his bad-boy looks on that cold night. I smiled over at him. "We missed the bus," I remember saying, hoping that he would talk.

He nodded, one finger latched over the knot in his tie as he loosened it, the smile lingering on his face as his eyes roved my body. "You're cold."

It was a statement more than a question, but I answered him, wanting him to talk to me some more. "Yes, aren't you?"

He shrugged. The hard man. His hair shone blue black in the streetlight, and I wanted to touch it. I found myself turning toward him, flirting even. "Do you work around here? I haven't seen you before."

"I came for an interview at Philpotts." He nodded back at the building he'd come from. His accent was South London. It made me smile. It made me feel warm inside.

Then he surprised me. He reached over to my face and stroked a clinging snowflake from my cheek. His touch sent a shiver through me, but this one was no cold shiver. He seemed to be aware of it and a sizzle passed between us, as real as a charge of electricity. "How long until the next bus?"

"About half an hour," I said, rubbing my gloved hands together. He lifted my hands in his, tugging off the gloves my mother had knitted and tucking them into my pockets before warming my hands inside his larger ones. The act was so strangely intimate, like something a lover would do. No man had ever touched me that way, especially not a stranger. Inside, something essentially female and desirous blossomed, and then quickly turned to liquid heat.

He put his head on one side, looking at me quizzically. "Do you want to go somewhere, to get warm?"

My heart thudded in response to the suggestion. I knew I probably shouldn't go anywhere with him, but curiosity and desire had a strong a grip on me.

He nodded again at Philpotts. "I know a place."

Between my thighs the most intimate part of me clenched. I rubbed my thighs together in response, but then pulled my hands away from his instinctively, unsure. Conflicting emotion ran in my blood. My fingers moved over the buttons on my coat, the same way that my hand closed over my pussy in my bed at night, dreaming of being taken in a man's arms, dreaming of having a man's hand right where mine strayed. "It's good," he added. "You'll like it."

I nodded.

He took my hand, leading me. Curiosity, fear and arousal assaulted my nerves as I lurched after him through the snow. His hand was large and solid, uncompromising as it enclosed mine. As we walked, I noticed how the falling snow muted the streetlamps, making the place seem hushed. It felt as if we were entirely alone. What was I doing? The only thing I knew for sure was that I wanted to follow where he led and have him make me warm.

He went as far as the Philpott building and then turned down the side of it. A security light on the corner of the building cast a wedge of light in either direction. Beyond that fall of light, where he was headed, it was gloomy and the snow drifted up against the wall. I paused, drawing him to a halt, too, my hand pulling free of his. "It's all right," he said, eyes twinkling when the light caught them. "There's a warm place here."

"I don't see it," I replied, still unsure.

"What's the matter? Don't you trust me?" He gave a wry smile, like he knew what I was thinking, but beckoned anyway.

Cautiously, I followed at a distance, until I saw him point over at the wall of the building. A large chimneystack jutted out from the brick wall, and the snow was melting away around the area, both on the nearby ground, and on the wall itself.

He moved over to the wall and put one hand against it. "You can warm yourself here. The furnace is inside, at the back of this wall."

Looking up, I saw smoke curling up from the stack, like steam in the sky. Further along the wall, snow still clung. Not there, not where the bricks were warm. He'd been serious, there really was somewhere warm here.

He hadn't meant...

I gave a soft chuckle when I stepped over and joined him against the wall. "Oh, that's good," I whispered when I felt the subtle warmth against the back of my frozen calf muscles. "I thought you meant something else," I added, before I thought through what I was saying. His mouth lifted and he cocked his head on one side. "Something else?" He put one elbow up against the wall and shuffled closer, until our bodies pressed alongside each other. "You thought I meant come down here for something else?"

His smile was wickedly suggestive, and I gave an embarrassed laugh, realizing what I'd revealed. But then he moved closer, growing serious, his hand stroking along my jaw to lift my face with one finger under my chin. "What something else where you thinking of, Missy?"

My feet shuffled nervously in the snow, my back shifting up against the wall. I glanced away from his stare—then back, compelled to look at him, even though I couldn't bring myself to reply to his question. He gave a dark chuckle, eyes on my lips, strong hand still holding my jaw. He bent and brushed his mouth over mine, barely, tantalizingly, making my lips hum with sensation. Breathless, I stared at him. "I think maybe you meant this kind of getting warm," he breathed, the back of his hand sliding down the surface of my throat.

A moan escaped me. Raw need roved my body, my nerve endings on high alert. When I didn't resist, his hand stole inside my coat, until it rested around the curve of my breast within my soft, knitted sweater. Part of me wanted to run, and yet part of me wanted to clutch at his coat and pull him nearer. My hands went flat against the rough bricks to stop myself snatching at him. My lust was like a caged creature, unsure about the open door being offered, and yet longing to find its freedom. But he was older, braver, and he knew what I wanted—what I needed, what I dreamed of alone in my bed at night.

His thumb stroked over the outline of my nipple through my sweater and bra. "Oh yes, this is what you wanted, isn't it?"

In his eyes, an accusing stare.

I nodded, my breast aching for more contact.

"Say it," he insisted.

I wriggled against the wall, pushing my breast into his hand. "Yes," I blurted. His hand explored me, sure and firm, squeezing the whole of my breast in his palm before moving down the outline of my waist and hip, until his fingertips reached the hem of my skirt. "You wanted a quick tumble to get your blood pumping, you bad girl."

The way he said "bad girl" made my stomach flip. Yes, I was being bad; I was being bad with him. I gasped aloud, inhaling deeply. He smelt of cheap cologne and cigarettes. He likely did this all the time, a quickie with a girl out back, but this time it was me, and I was fiercely glad of it. His touch through my stockings was almost painful on the frozen skin of my thighs. Each stroke he made with his hand was echoed by a pang of need in my pussy. My breath was already coming in quick pants. I reached for him, my hands trembling, eager yet jittery. He paused when he reached the top of my stocking, roving back and forth across it, moving around its edge to the clasp on my garter belt, plucking at it, his hand nudging up under my skirt. When I moaned against his face, he put his hand under the belt, spreading it around my thigh.

Inside his biker jacket I could feel the lean outline of his torso beneath the crisp white shirt he wore. My fingers stole under the tie and between two buttons, desperate to touch his skin.

His hand curved around the mound of my pussy through my cotton underwear, and it seemed to be the perfect size to hold me there—hold me firm. I whimpered and pressed myself into the precious cup of his willing hand. His eyes narrowed in response, and I could tell he was aroused, too, his body taut against mine. "Getting warmer now?" He sounded amused.

Heat flared in my face, and I nodded. My breath felt trapped in my throat, every cold intake a vivid contrast to the heat inside. When his middle finger moved, pressing the soft fabric of my underwear into my damp niche, my legs felt weak and my head dropped back against the wall, hair catching on its rough surface.

"You're very hot in here," he said, with an accusing chuckle.

I was unable to answer, because my body was moving, responding to the stimulation he was giving me. I was rising and falling in his hand, and each time I did, pleasure shot from my clit, right through my groin. "You made me hot," I blurted suddenly, blushing when I heard my own voice, yet silently begging him for more—for release.

He knew what I wanted. He looked into my eyes as he pushed his hand into my underwear and touched me there.

"Oh, oh," I whimpered. I felt pinned by his stare, opened up by his fingers, my intimate folds tingling with sensation as he explored them.

He was bold, his finger sliding over my dampness, teasing

my inflamed clit as he stroked the length of my slit, over and over again, until my back was moving against the wall, one foot lifted from the ground, my inner thigh against the outside of his.

My hand brushed over his belt buckle, lower, to the bulky shape beneath his fly. He made a sound like a growl in his throat when my hand moved over his erection, his eyes closing for a moment. Then he acted on it and undid the top buttons on his fly, inviting me in, a sly grin on his face.

Could I touch him? I pushed back my tumbling hair with one shaking hand, scared, but acting on instinct. I slid my palm around the head of his cock, marveling at how hot it was, then moved lower, tightening on the shaft as I moved my hand up and down, exploring it under the cover of his dangling shirttails. Its rigidity and smoothness startled me, starting a new wave of lust, making my pussy clench and my back undulate.

"That's good," he growled under his breath. "Oh yeah... you're going to make me come." He reached lower, stroked a damp smear of my juices up to my clit and centered his fingertip there, rolling over it, back and forth, quick but gentle, almost teasing. And my hand stroked the hot shaft of his cock up and down in response, up and down, until he got even harder, and I saw him grit his teeth and lift his chin.

The heat was building inside me, fast, and the oncoming climax felt heavy and powerful. I wondered vaguely at the back of my mind if my legs would buckle. I heard myself let out a mewling sound, almost lost to the moment. At my back, the heat coming through the wall was like an echo of the startling, raw fire he'd unleashed between my legs, a climax closing like none I'd ever given myself—all-encompassing, hot and wild. It

•

made me tremble from top to tail, grunts of acknowledgment escaping my lips as he stared into my eyes, urging me on, and as I burned and spilled in his hand, his cock lurched in mine and he spurted against the tails of his crisp, white, interview shirt. He moved closer as he did up his fly, letting my skirt drop. He pressed fully against me, nestling into the spoon of my hips, closing our shared heat in between us, savoring it. I don't remember how long it was, but we were still breathing fast and huddled together, kissing, touching, exploring, when I heard the distant sound of wheels through the snow and saw the headlights lighting up the street. "The bus," I said, "hurry."

We straightened our clothes and ran, out into the street, arms waving, the pair of us falling onto the bus, laughing, glad of it and of each other. And then in the crowded vehicle we grew quiet and smiled across at each other as I attempted to tidy my hair and put my gloves back on, sharing the silent secret of what we had done together back there by the furnace. His stop came first, and he waved and winked at me as he left the bus. After he'd gone, my secret smile stayed with me, as did the physical memory, that first time becoming an essential part of my female self.

I never saw him again. I figured he never got the job that he was being interviewed for. I wondered often enough about what the job was, something to do with the furnace? How else would he have known? Whenever anyone I knew came out of the Philpotts factory I quizzed them at the bus stop. But no one seemed to know him.

How could they not remember him?

I never forgot.

I didn't even know his name, but somehow that didn't matter. For months following that night I would touch myself at night and think only of him as I fell asleep. Often, I'd wake in a sweat, my clit throbbing after dreaming of his body naked and hard between my thighs, just as his clever fingers had been that night, as if in haunting my body he gave me the key to a vast chamber of fantasy, my passion liberated from that moment on.

And now, years later, I'm a successful businesswoman, and a mother, powerful in my own right, but that essential foundation of my liberated female self is still treasured. The physical memory never fails to warm me all over again. I can picture his smile; feel his touch—the bad boy in the virgin snow, the first man to make me come. It taught me to expect the unexpected in life. It taught me that passion can be found and shared in the most unusual of places, and that the memory of a captured moment of pure, shared passion between two people can last a lifetime.

YOU CAN DO MINE

Cerise Noire

I can't believe I'm actually getting to do this, I
thought as I watched my purple jelly cock enter his ass.

From the time I lost my virginity to a well-
hung—and none too skilled—high school boy,
I realized the need for a way to keep my ass
safe from intrusion. It isn't so much that I was
opposed to the idea of anal sex, just that all the
guys who ever asked did so with such a sense
of entitlement that I felt they weren't worthy
of it. It was always about their pleasure, about
how tight it would feel for them, never about
me. So when that first high school boy tried to
discreetly slip into that puckered hole of mine,
I came up with the phrase that would keep my
ass safe for many years:

"You can do mine, if I can do yours."

This usually got me reactions ranging from shock and horror to nervous laughter. In any case, it always turned out to be enough to keep my ass out of cock's way. At least it did until I met Leo.

It was one of those days when I'd chosen to sit at my local library, ignoring the pile of papers waiting to be graded back at home. I had claimed my usual spot on the floor, at the back of the 800s section; it seemed to always be the most deserted. I was immersed in my umpteenth rereading of Camus' *L'Étranger*, when a smooth, deep voice broke through my bibliophile's trance.

"Excuse me, mind if I get that?"

A graceful hand pointed at a book on one of the bottom shelves I was apparently blocking. I picked up the obscure volume on Italian medieval satire, and handed it to the owner of the gorgeous hand. As I did so, I looked up into a pair of green eyes framed by heavy black lashes. His hair was a disorderly mass of shiny black waves that fell to his shoulders. The stranger's face was of the same golden shade as the hand that had first caught my attention. It was the perfect backdrop for the full, sinful lips curved in an amused smirk. I was staring.

"Oh...um...here you go," I stammered, waving the book about like a complete idiot.

He ignored it and squatted in front of me, cocking his head to read the title of my book and then snatching it right out of my hand. He settled on the floor, cross-legged, leaving barely a couple of inches between us. I didn't remember asking for company.

"Excuse me," I started in my stern teacher voice. "What do you think you're—?"

"Reading it in the original French," he said, unimpressed by my attempt at authority. "How interesting." He walked away with my book. I followed him.

We ended up sitting in a tiny coffee shop and, after exchanging names, comparing views on various European authors. When Leo mentioned the subtle Sapphic symbolism found in a Celtic poem he had been studying, I knew I would end up having sex with him. What can I say? Alliteration makes me wet. Or maybe it was the fact that I hadn't had sex with anyone in over five years. In any case, two bottles of wine later, I stood and threw a few bills on the table.

"I have to get home now," I said as I started walking away. Then I looked at him over my shoulder. "Well, are you coming?" This time, after adding some cash to mine, he followed.

We got to my apartment, which looked the same as always. There was a pile of books next to the couch, another on the coffee table, and a thick tome on word histories on the breakfast counter. In one corner, my desk disappeared under papers still waiting to be corrected, my PC almost dwarfed by their abundance. Despite the mess, there was no dust anywhere, and I could catch a glimpse of my freakishly organized closet over in the bedroom. Somehow, I didn't think he would care. From our conversation, I had learned that he was one of those career students, living the so-called bohemian life. In other words, he was well read and unemployed. That ruled him out as a prospective boyfriend, but it didn't keep me from wanting to eat him. Or wanting him to eat me.

I settled for taking a bite. I stepped up to him, pulled his face down to mine, and bit his lower lip. He chuckled, pulled back, and caressed my face, looking at me as if we'd been lovers for years. He kissed me, his lips barely brushing against mine at first. He traced my lips with the tip of his tongue, before letting it slip in. I softened as he drew me in, holding me tighter in his arms. I closed my eyes. I was lost in the sweet cloves and coffee taste of his mouth.

He swept me off my feet—literally. I squealed; with my solid thighs, ample bottom, and heavy breasts, I'm not the kind of girl who gets to be carried very often. I wrapped my legs around his waist and tangled his hair around my fingers. I bit at the skin of his neck while he walked us to the bedroom.

I kissed him harder, tugging at his hair until he faltered. We crashed onto the bedroom carpet, yet our lips remained locked. His hand slipped under my shirt, squeezing my lace-covered breasts until my hardened nipples poked right through the holes in the pattern.

Leo pulled his face away from mine. A cry of protest died in my throat when he removed my shirt and captured one nipple between his lips. He sucked and licked as I arched my back, feeding him more of my breast. He turned his attention from one breast to the other, kneading the breast that was not being caressed by his tongue.

He looked up at me and smiled, before sliding down to pull off my pants. He blew on the skin of my inner thighs, and I trembled. He nibbled at the back of my knees, licked at the crease between my thigh and my sex, and just as I thought that he would remove my panties, he slid up to kiss me hard on the mouth again.

With only a layer of lace covering my pussy, the grinding of Leo's pelvis against mine was torture. I rolled us over until I was sitting on that tantalizing bulge. I bit at Leo's neck, rubbing against him as I listened to his ragged breath. I shifted down to get his cock out of his jeans and noticed the wet spot I'd left on his crotch. As soon as I undid the fly, Leo's cock

sprang up, bumping against my lips. I might have guessed he'd
be too bohemian for underwear.

His cock looked too tempting for me to wait, and I slipped
the head between my lips as I continued to pull down his
jeans. I couldn't get them past his knees without letting go of
his cock, so I left them bunched up halfway down. Leo sat up,
resting his back against the bed. I swallowed more of his cock,
until the head tickled the opening of my throat. Leo moaned
and placed his hand on the back of my head, not pushing, but
simply stroking my hair.

He pulled me off of him, stood, and stepped out of his pants.
I sat on the edge of the bed, rubbing myself through my panties while his shirt joined the clothes on the floor. My mouth
watered at the sight of his creamy butterscotch skin.

Leo knelt in front of me and hooked his thumbs under the
sides of my panties, before pulling then down my legs. This
time, he dove in with a long lick from the bottom of my slit
to just below the engorged bud of my clit. He licked his lips
and looked at me, hunger in his eyes, before grabbing my ass
and placing my legs over his shoulders. He took a deep whiff
of my musk, and then pulled each swollen lip into his mouth.
His tongue snaked into every sensitive fold of my pussy, making me whimper and squirm against his face.

He clamped his lips around my clit and fed on me, holding me fast as I bucked, lost in my own pleasure. My muscles tightened, and then relaxed all at once as I came with a
scream. He sucked lazily until my body settled. He stood, letting my feet fall back to the floor.

"Tasty," he said as he joined me on the bed. He kissed me,
as if to support his claim. He was right. I was tasty.

I turned to rummage through my nightstand for a condom.

Leo took it out of my hand and unrolled it on his cock. I lay on my back and spread my thighs. He slid into me. I gasped. He thrust in and out slowly, letting me feel every inch of his cock against the walls of my pussy.

Soon, Leo increased his speed, banging his pelvis against mine. The room smelled like sex, and we were beyond words now, our grunts and moans almost drowning out the sound of his cock sliding in my juices. I clawed at his back. He held me close, so that the rubbing of his groin against mine electrified my clit more than I could bear. I came again, with a drawn-out wail that made my earlier cry seem discreet.

I fell back with a sigh, too exhausted to move. Leo slid out of me, and I quivered at the sudden emptiness. I looked down. He was still hard.

"Oh," I said, "you didn't..."

Leo shook his head. I sat up and reached out for his cock. He waved my hand away.

"Don't worry," he said. He got up and came around to my side of the bed. "Go to sleep, beautiful." He kissed my forehead.

I watched his muscular ass flex as he walked into the bathroom, before I closed my eyes, too tired to stay awake.

I woke up with Leo's arm around me, his hand holding one of my breasts. I looked at the clock: 5:30. I moved Leo's hand, careful not to wake him, and he rolled over to his back, causing the sheet to fall to the floor. I stood and looked back at his peaceful form before heading for the bathroom. It had been ages since I'd brought a man home, let alone one this gorgeous. It was just the kind of one-night stand I needed to clean out the cobwebs.

I showered, and when I came out, Leo was still sleeping. I placed one hand on his shoulder.

"Hey, um, I need to go to work soon," I said.

"Uh, Okay." He stirred. I hoped he would be up by the time I finished breakfast.

I went to the kitchen for a cup of coffee, and I popped two frozen waffles into the toaster. Once full, I walked back to my closet for some clothes. Leo was out of bed, but he was in the shower.

"Hey Leo," I yelled toward the bathroom door, "I'm leaving in five minutes." He didn't hear me, and the door was locked. I gathered my lesson plans, my purse, and my laptop, and set them by the door. If I waited any longer, I'd be late for work. I scribbled a note thanking him for the previous night, and asking him to engage the lock before he closed the door on his way out.

Before I left for work, I checked the bedroom again. He was still in the shower, singing an old-fashioned love song.

When I came home that evening, I smelled something appetizing as soon as I approached the door. I walked in to find that the dining table was covered with a fancy tablecloth I'd forgotten I owned. Leo was in front of the stove, stirring the contents of a pot.

"Hey, Céline, you're home." He covered the pot. He poured a glass of wine and handed it to me. "Here, relax. The food's almost done."

Apparently the meaning of my note had been lost on him. He hadn't left.

Three months later, Leo still had not left. Somehow I had gone from my single woman's routine to having a live-in boyfriend. That is if one defines "live-in boyfriend" as a man who shares the bed and spends most of his days reading obscure books on my couch. At least he cooked, and he had managed to charm my landlady into pretending she hadn't noticed the extra tenant. He would leave on occasion, presumably for a change of clothes, and always before I woke up.

This particular Friday was one such occasion, and when I opened my eyes, I found a scrap of paper on his pillow, with three lines of his ornate handwriting.

One thousand kisses
will rain on your skin tonight
when we meet again

I slipped the note between the pages of my journal before getting out of bed. In the kitchen, I found fresh fruit, cereal, and a glass of orange juice waiting for me. There was another note on the counter, a single coral rose laid across it.

Céline
luscious, soft
moaning, writhing, coming
the tastiest of treats
lover

I smiled and picked up the phone.

"Hello? Anna? It's Céline. Look, can you squeeze me in for a Brazilian during my lunch break? Twelve to twelve thirty?" I paused while Anna checked her appointment book. "You can?

Great, thanks, I owe you one. See you then."

I ate my meal and hopped in the shower. Maybe I would buy some new panties on the way home from work.

Once back at my apartment, I tried to grade some papers while I waited for Leo. I gave up after half an hour; I couldn't concentrate. Just as I placed the rest of the papers back on my desk, the phone rang. It was Leo. He wanted to let me know he needed to take care of a few things over there—wherever "there" was—and that he would be here soon.

I hung up, and went to the bedroom to change before his arrival.

After I changed, I waited for Leo at the window, and called his name when he reached the front of the building.

"Come on up," I said, waving.

I didn't move from my spot at the window when he came in, but the sound of his bag dropping to the floor told me that he approved of my choice of clothing. Unable to make up my mind about what to wear, I had chosen a pair of red heels—and nothing else.

He walked to my side and caressed my skin from the nape of my neck to the bottom of my back.

"Hi, Love," he said. "You just get more gorgeous every day, don't you?" He turned me around and kissed me.

"Wait," I said, pulling away from him, "don't you want to have dinner first?"

He looked at me with one raised eyebrow.

"So, you dressed like this for dinner?" he asked.

I shook my head and went to lie on the couch. Leo took off his T-shirt and sat on the carpet in front of me. He rested his cheek on my chest, and I held him in my arms as he suckled my nipple. He caressed my side, stopping to grab a handful of my ass. He kneaded the flesh there, yet did not let go of my breast.

Leo sat up and pulled me down until I was kneeling in front of the couch, my face pressed into the cushions where I could smell a faint trace of my juices. Leo trailed his hands over the back of my thighs before spreading my cheeks. He rubbed his nose along the bare length of my lips, and then followed the same path with his tongue.

"Mm, smooth," he said.

He teased my wet flesh with the tip of his tongue as I writhed under his attention. He grabbed me by the waist, flipped me over, and without giving me time to catch my breath, latched on to my clit. I moaned. With my clit still trapped between his lips, he slipped two fingers into the slick heat of my pussy. All feeling in my body focused there, around his fingers, as my inner muscles contracted. Just when I relaxed enough for him to withdraw his fingers, he pulled them out and thrust them in my ass. I froze—then my body shook as I groaned through a second orgasm.

Leo took his fingers out of me and kissed me, his erection hard against my belly. He repositioned himself and nudged at the puckered hole below my slit with the head of his cock. I flinched and pushed his shoulders back until he lay supine.

I turned my back to him, straddled him and sank onto his cock. My hips ground against him, and he groaned each time I flexed my pussy around him. God, I loved the way he filled me when I was on top. I bounced on his cock, holding my breath every time he bottomed out. Leo rose to his knees, his arm around my waist so that I wouldn't lose my balance. He thrust into me frantically, and I bucked back against him. I teased my clit with my fingers, until my insides tingled. He pulled out and rested the head of his twitching cock atop the seam of my ass. He groaned, and his cum trickled down into the hole his fingers had stretched. When his tongue followed the milky trail, the tension between my legs exploded.

We lay on the floor, our limbs tangled, while our breaths returned to normal.

"Céline," Leo said once his heartbeat settled to a near-resting pace.

"Hm?"

"You didn't let me..." He ran his finger down the cleft of my ass.

"You didn't ask."

"Well, can I? Next time?"

"It depends," I said, looking him in the eyes. "You can do mine—if I can do yours."

He untangled his legs from mine, huffed, and looked away. He stood.

"I'm going to the bathroom," he said before walking away.

When Leo reentered the living room, I had on a robe, and I was warming up leftover takeout for us. He sat at the counter and traced invisible lines on the surface with his fingertips. I walked over to the fridge.

"What do you want to drink," I asked without looking up.

"Okay."

I straightened up and turned around.

"What?"

"Okay. Let's do it. You—you can do me."

My eyes widened as the meaning of his words became clear. I'd used that proposition for years, but no guy had ever considered it, let alone agreed. I pondered the possibilities for a moment. I nodded.

"All right," I said, "and then you can do me."

We discussed the details over dinner, and soon we were huddled in front of my PC screen, looking up and ordering the necessary materials.

"How about this one?" I pointed at a rubber cock the size of the water bottle I carried to work.

He looked at me, eyes wide and mouth agape.

"Um, that's a bit much. I was thinking of a more, um, even exchange." He pointed at another area of the screen. "How about this one? It's about the same size as my dick."

"Yeah, I guess that would be fair."

"It would," he said, "and it's purple, your favorite color."

A few more clicks for a thong-style harness and some lube, and we were ready for overnight delivery. Good thing the next day was Saturday. There was no way I could have concentrated at work all day with thoughts of that package in the mail.

Leo and I slept in. Around eleven, we made our way to the kitchen for coffee. We lounged on the couch, watching Saturday morning cartoons and exchanging few words besides mundane chitchat.

The doorbell rang.

We looked at each other, neither of us moving at first. I stood and walked to the door. It was the delivery man. I signed for the package. Leo followed me to the bedroom, and watched as I opened the box. We unwrapped each item, the rubber-smelling dildo, the pump-bottle of lube, and the pliant leather harness, and there we were again, staring and motionless.

I took Leo's hand and led him to the bathroom. I removed

the pajama top I had on, and Leo did the same with the matching bottoms he wore. I stepped into the shower and pulled him in after me. I turned on the water, reached for the shampoo, and squeezed some into the palm of my hand.

"Turn around," I said. I washed his hair, stretching up to massage his scalp through the cleansing lather. I rinsed it off, noticing how the black mass now fell below his shoulder blades.

I poured shower gel onto a washcloth. I reached around Leo's body to soap his torso, pressing my chest against his back rather than having him turn around. I avoided his cock, turning my attention to his back instead. I lifted his hair, holding it in one hand while I soaped his back. It fell against his skin with a wet smack as I soaped my way down to his ass. I abandoned the washcloth, using my hand instead to work the lather into the skin, kneading the muscular flesh. Kneeling behind him, I trailed my soapy hand down the crevice of his ass. He shivered.

Leo turned around and held his hand out to me. He pulled me up into his arms and kissed me. He didn't bother with a washcloth, but instead poured the shower gel directly into his hand. He spread it down my back, and when he reached my ass, he grabbed each cheek and pressed me against him. I moaned.

He stepped back and looked at me.

"We're soapy," he said. He looked down at his erection. "But you forgot something.

He spun me around so that my back was to him, and once I placed my hands flat on the tiled wall for support, he slipped his cock between my soapy thighs. He slid back and forth, the friction against my lips making my juices flow and blend with the water.

"Let's go," I said, backing us up until we stood under the

showerhead. I took his hand once more and led him back to the bedroom.

Leo sat on the bed. I knelt on the floor, between his legs, and I licked his cock from root to tip and back. I sucked his balls into my mouth, focusing on one, then the other, before spreading his knees a little further and rimming his puckered hole with the tip of my tongue. He seemed to open for me, and soon my tongue was darting in and out of him, while my fingers mirrored its rhythm, in and out of my pussy.

I pulled the slick digits from my own wetness and slipped one into his hole. This time, Leo clenched against the intrusion, before relaxing again with a sigh. I wriggled my fingers, watching him squirm while I pushed them in him. The head of his cock darkened to a deep crimson.

I stood. Leo stared while I affixed the dildo to the harness and fastened myself into the leather straps. I pumped a generous amount of lube into my hands and stroked my new appendage, moaning at the thought of what was to come. I applied the excess lube to his hole, before positioning the tip of my cock there.

I looked at him and waited. He took a deep breath, pulled his knees up toward his chest, and nodded.

I pushed forward.

I can't believe I'm actually getting to do this, I thought as I watched my purple jelly cock enter his ass.

He winced when the head popped in. His cock twitched.

I waited for him to adjust to my girth, and then I sank into him, bit by bit. This time he groaned and grabbed his cock. He stroked it in sync with my thrusts, groaning each time my balls touched his cheeks. Our breaths became ragged as my rhythm crescendoed.

Leo's bellowing cry caught me by surprise when he came.

Perhaps it was the image of him smiling, his own cum splattered all over his hard stomach. Perhaps it was looking at my cock still lodged in his ass. Or maybe the leather strap splitting my pussy had teased me past my limit. Whatever it was, I came soon after him. I pulled out and collapsed into his arms.

When I opened my eyes again, Leo was looking at me and, stroking himself back to hardness. He reached around me, grabbed my ass, and then smacked it.

"Your turn," he said. He licked his lips and reached for the bottle of lube.

I rolled onto my belly, looked over my shoulder, and smiled.

BLAME

Amy Wadhams

I am not ashamed of what I did. People may condemn me for it, but I can't be sorry I did it. As I look back across the years, it is a sweet memory. The aftermath was unfortunate, but still, I cherish the remembrance. I will tell you my story and see if you can castigate me.

It was a rainy summer, and all the children were tormenting their parents. Mothers peeked wistfully between curtains wishing for a day dry enough to send the kids outside to play. I had just graduated college, and was back at home and drifting. I was a twenty-four-year-old teenager.

My dad kept urging me to look for a job. He'd slap a newspaper before me at the breakfast table as I groggily spooned cereal in the general direction of my mouth, and grunt,

"There are some good prospects in there for accountants. I didn't pay for all that college for nothing." Too bad I hated accounting. Since they were shelling out so much cash for said college education, my parents had felt that they should choose my major.

I'd wanted to do something artistic. I'd always had a flair for art and music. I wanted more than a brain-numbing job crunching numbers, a boring husband, and two-point-four kids. All through college I'd gritted my teeth through the coma-inducing lectures, and fulfilled my need for expression with poetry club, experimental drug use, body modification, and sleeping my way through every band that played in the local rock scene.

It wasn't a past that I was proud of, but it was typical of a sheltered, small-town rebel finally on her own in the big city. So, there I was, trying to aim a spoonful of breakfast at my face with my eyes crusted shut, and expecting good ol' Dad to pull the newspaper routine, when Mom said, "Leslie, I got a call from your Aunt Shauna last night. She's had an idea." I dragged my eyes open warily. "Aunt" Shauna wasn't really my aunt. She was my mom's best friend from the beginning of time, and she had grown to heartily disapprove of my riotous ways and manner of dress.

Therefore I was rightfully mistrustful of any ideas she might have about me. My mom rolled her eyes and huffed, "Don't look like that, she has your best interests at heart. She's known you since you were born, and cares about you." I rolled my eyes and didn't bother reminding her that Shauna practically wanted to douse me in holy water and chant, "The power of Christ compels you," every time we met. She was constantly urging me to lose the punk-goth look and come to church with her. I told her if her church wouldn't have me because of my appearance then they weren't any church I wanted to attend.

Then she would tell me quietly that she would pray for me. And I'd put on my Mother Teresa face and reply sanctimoniously that I'd pray for her as well. So, yeah, we weren't great friends. Mom sighed and continued, "Shauna thought that you might come up to Houston and stay with her and Sonny for a while, and see if you could find a job there. She thought it might break you out of your funk." Sonny was Shauna's son, six years my junior, and as far as I remembered he had a bigger stick up his ass than his mom.

But being back in the city rather than here in the hot, sticky armpit of the Texas gulf coast sounded like heaven. I shook myself fully awake, which took a few minutes, it being the ungodly hour of eight in the morning. I thought it over, weighing the desirability of being in Houston against the aggravation of putting up with Shauna and Sonny. I decided that I didn't need to spend much time with them, so Houston won out.

That afternoon, I was flying up highway 288 in my battered old Ford, pounding my fist on the steering wheel in time with the pumping rock blasting from my speakers. The hazy skyline of Houston grew before me, and my spirits lifted with the tips of the skyscrapers. I exited just inside the Loop, and wound through the maze of one-way streets until I found Shauna's apartment complex. I pulled into the parking space she'd told me to use, checked the sooty eyeliner I'd rimmed my eyes with earlier, then grabbed my bag and jumped out, yanking my black tank top lower over the waistband of my jeans.

The sidewalk was so hot I thought the soles of my Chuck Taylors would melt to it. I merrily jingled my handcuff belt buckle with the hand that wasn't carrying a suitcase. I skipped up the stairs to drop my luggage in front of apartment number 1372, and pushed the buzzer. The blinds next to the door flicked and I saw Shauna's gray eyes peeking out anxiously. Then the blinds fell back into place, and I heard the sound of locks opening. Lots of locks. I rolled my eyes.

The door opened and Shauna whisked me inside, securing the locks again after me. I smiled and said, "You aren't supposed to look out the windows, Aunt Shauna. The bad guys would know you're here, and have a target." She frowned and said, "Leslie, why must you always be so contentious?" I smiled wider and thought, *You just bring out the best in me, Auntie dear.* I gave myself grown-up points for not saying it out loud.

She picked up my bag, glancing at my attire, and waved me down the hall, saying over her shoulder, "You will have the guest room, dear. I'm afraid Sonny is out at the moment. He is looking forward to seeing you again."

Yeah, right, I thought. He was probably passing out religious tracts at abortion clinics or something. I followed her into the guest room, and wrinkled my nose. I'd never seen so much pink and ruffles. So not me.

She heaved my bag onto the bed, and told me to go ahead and unpack while she made dinner. I made a face at her retreating back, then unzipped the suitcase and threw open the lid. I began unpacking, putting my clothes in the closet, and scattering my odd trinkets around the room. When I exited the room, the smell of sizzling pork chops lured me into the kitchen. Shauna asked me to set two places at the table.

I opened a cabinet, looking for plates, and asked, "Two places? What about Sonny?" A small crease appeared between her brows as she studied the pork chops, a look usually reserved for me, and said quietly, "He won't be back in time. He keeps late hours." My eyebrows rose. So, Mister Church Boy was doing something Mommy Dearest didn't approve of. I did a quick mental calculation and figured he should be about eighteen now. Just about the age when I started to seriously rebel.

"Good for you, Sonny" I thought, and began to look forward to seeing him. Though, knowing the two of them, all he was doing was watching R-rated movies, or reading naughty books in the library. I set the table and had a thoroughly uncomfortable dinner with "Aunt" Shauna.

When I went to bed, after declining her offer to watch the Christian channel with her, I planned the next day. I would sleep in, foregoing my loving father's seven thirty wake-up time demand. Then I would go out at about two in the afternoon to "find a job." Meaning I was going to look up some old buddies. The tiny southeast Texas town my family lived in hadn't had men in my flavor of moody, and I'd been without sex for too long.

Lying in bed, I closed my eyes and pictured the gorgeous specimen of a lead singer I planned to ferret out the next day. I drifted off to sleep with visions of leather-clad S/M gods dancing in my head.

The next morning did not go quite as I had planned. Shauna crept into my bedroom and prodded me awake at the hour of seven. She told me she was leaving for work, and she needed me to wake up so I could let Sonny in when he got home. It drifted through my sleep-fogged brain that Sonny had spent the whole night out. Something was going on.

I pried myself out of bed, and trudged down the hall to collapse on the couch under the front window. I grunted in response to her hurried thanks, and flipped on the TV as she left, telling me to lock all the locks. I glanced up at the door and decided that I'd rather risk an intruder than be upright again. As I found a cartoon to watch, I pulled the ugly knitted afghan from the top of the couch to cover my black T-shirt and panties.

I drifted off almost immediately. Odd dreams floated through my rest, until the sound of a shrill bell jarred me awake. Flinging my hand out to pound the offending noisemaker into silence, I hit a telephone, and realized that it was the source of the racket. I hauled the receiver to my ear and managed, "'Lo?"

"Hello," a voice answered in a questioning tone. There was loud background noise, music and people's voices. "Who is this?" the voice continued. I moaned and rolled over, then forced out, "This is Leslie. Who the fuck is this?" A pause followed, then the voice replied, "Leslie? This is Sonny. Why are you answering our phone?"

I groaned loudly, annoyed, and said, "Because your dear mother got me up to wait for your ass to get home while she went to work."

"Oh," he responded. "Well, I'm going to be home in about five minutes. I'm bringing a few friends with me."

"Great," I muttered. "Just keep the prayer meeting or whatever the hell it is quiet, because I'm tired of getting woken up."

Humor infused his voice as he said, "Yeah, okay. Prayer meeting. Right." Then he hung up without saying good-bye.

I looked at the phone and growled as I hung it up, "Rude little bastard." Then I rolled over and dropped back off into slumber. Only to be woken again by the sound of pounding on the door. Emitting a loud snarl of displeasure, I flung the afghan off me and jumped up. I yanked the door open, not even opening my eyes, and plopped back down on the couch, grumbling, "The fucker was unlocked. Jesus, can't a person get a decent sleep around here?"

I heard several voices laughing, and I realized that my T-shirt had ridden up and my legs were completely sprawled open, giving Sonny and his buddies a free shot of my black bikini undies and thorough wax job. Groaning again, I reached blindly for the afghan, and covered myself, muttering, "You bunch of pervs."

Then a coarse, rich, butterscotch voice said, "My mom would flip if she knew you didn't lock the door."

My eyebrows drew together slightly, as I realized the owner of the touchable, sexy voice must be Sonny. Slowly, I hefted one eyelid slightly to peek at him, then fully opened both eyes as I took in the view. There stood Sonny, surrounded by a group of young people in every shade of black clothing. Sonny did not look a damn thing like I remembered. The Sonny I remembered had the look that said, "Beat me up, please." This Sonny; well, let's just say it was a far cry.

His hair was long, brushing his shoulders, and dyed raven black. He wore a black shirt and black jeans that hugged his lanky young frame. His full mouth was pierced on either side of his lower lip, silver gleaming from the loops. His nose was almost too large, as if he were still growing into it. Dark brown eyes shone from their rim of black eyeliner. The eyes caught me, there was such liveliness and expression shining from their depths.

I opened my mouth a few times, trying to form a sentence, and finally accomplished, "What the hell happened to you, Church Boy?" His friends laughed, and he blushed. A girl I hadn't really noticed before clutched his arm tighter, glaring at me. Probably for almost flashing the guy she was obviously into. Sonny said, "Well, I couldn't let my mom dress me forever, huh?" I looked at him skeptically, then groused, "I guess. Whatever. I'm going back to sleep. Your mother is damned evil for waking me up at dark thirty."

They all laughed again, the sound grating on my nerves. Nearly screaming in my morning grouchiness, I stood up, not caring anymore who caught a glimpse of what, and gritted out, "I'm going back to that pink hellhole since you guys seem not to understand the meaning of shut the hell up. And where the blasted fuck is the thermostat?" I was near sweating, even in my minimal clothing. I continued, "It's like a goddamned sauna in here." As I entered my room, I pulled off my shirt, turned and threw it at them, then slammed the door.

The next thing I knew, I was being wakened by a light rap at the door. I rolled over and glanced at the clock on the bedside table. It was noon. Much better. Yawning and stretching, I said, "Who is it?"

"Sonny," he answered. "Can I come in? I wanted to talk to you."

"Yeah," I called, pulling the sheets up to cover my nude breasts. The door opened, and he came in and plopped down in the chair next to the bed. I rolled to my side, tucking the blanket around me, the top of my breasts peeking out, decorated with tattoos.

Sonny's eyes took in the slice of body art, then were quickly averted. He cleared his throat and said, "I'd appreciate it if you didn't tell my mom I had those people here. She doesn't really like them."

I chuckled in my gritty morning voice and said, "She

doesn't like me either, so don't worry about it. So, what happened to you? Last I remember you were Church Boy McPoindexter."

He smiled and leaned closer. "Don't you like the new me better? I guess I just grew up. I discovered some great music, and a great scene."

Trying to grasp the turnaround in my reality, I stared at him, taking in the black polish on his nails, the manly lines of his thick hands, and the way they lay on the taut fabric of his jeans. I had to remind myself that he was only eighteen. "So, chickipoo that was with your buddies earlier…was she your girlfriend, or the communal fuckbuddy for your little group?"

He frowned and thought for a moment, then said, "I guess she's a little of both. She's been with most of the guys, but she wants to date me. I'm not really into her."

"Don't like seconds?" I asked, grinning.

He smiled and said, "I don't mind experience, but I know where she's been, and where my friends she's slept with have been. I want no part of that."

"So," I asked, "no girlfriend?"

He looked down at his hands and murmured, "Not really. I've dated, but I've never…well, you know."

I must admit, that didn't surprise me. "Once a Church Boy, always a Church Boy," I chuckled.

He glanced back up at my face, then cleared his throat again. "It's not like I don't want to. I'm just…nervous, I guess. I don't know what I'm doing."

I laughed and said gently, "You've got to learn some time."

His eyes met mine, with a speculative light dancing in their bright depths. He slowly said, "What about you?"

I rolled onto my back and laughed heartily. "What about me? I'm not a virgin." I quieted down. "Far from it," I said softly.

"That's what I mean," he interjected quickly. "You know what you're doing."

He stood up and walked to the window, agitated, then turned slowly, came back, and sat on the edge of the bed, catching my gaze intently. He said hoarsely, "Will you teach me?"

I sat up hastily, grasping the blanket to my chest, and said, "What? You mean...you don't mean... Sonny, you've only just turned eighteen. I'm twenty-four!"

He said abruptly, "It wouldn't be illegal." His voice lowered, growing velvety. "Please, Leslie. I want you to teach me. I've wanted you for years, since I knew what wanting was. I'm not asking for a relationship, or anything. I know you're too old for me. But just teach me, let me get my first experience from you."

I sat immobilized by his words. This was the boy I used to alternately ignore and make fun of. But this was also an attractive young man, his sexuality just dawning. A game of mental tug-of-war was going on inside me. I had gone so long without the intimate touch of another human being, and here was a tempting, inexperienced man asking me to lead him into the land of carnal delights. The decision was already made, but I fought against it.

"Sonny," I began, "even if I agreed to this, my...predilections are not quite the norm. What I enjoy in bed tends to scare off most people. I don't think you need someone like me to introduce you to sex."

His eyes darkened, and he leaned closer, asking, "What do you like? I'm not scared to try anything. That's why I've wanted you for so long. With you I knew it wouldn't be boring normal intercourse."

I licked my lips, my mouth becoming more and more dry, then whispered, "You'd have to have a strong stomach. I like to be bitten. I like to be cut. I like pain."

He leaned even closer, his face inches from mine now, and said very softly, "Let me do that. I want to do that for you." He must have seen the answer in my eyes. He lifted one of his broad hands, and clenched the blanket in a fist and slowly pulled it away from my body.

My breathing hitched, as his stare lowered to my breasts. He lightly traced the tattoo of a skull on the top of my right breast; my eyes fluttered shut and my head fell back, allowing his hand to travel up to my neck. His thumb settled over my pulse, and with a sudden roughness that had my pussy clenching, he pulled me forward and attacked my lips with his, the very lightest hint of stubble on his face giving the kiss an eloquent edge of sensation.

His tongue slid past my lips to entwine with mine in a brutal dance as sensual as any intercourse, and his hands slid to my hips, yanking them to him, causing me to lie back. Our mouths parted, and with a predatory fierceness in his gleaming eyes, he tugged his shirt over his head revealing a wiry, lean torso. "Hmm," I said, "you seem to be doing fine without any instruction from me."

He smiled powerfully, and growled, "I've had plenty of time to imagine how I wanted to do this to you."

I reached out and began loosening the buckle of his studded belt. He pulled it off, and went to toss it aside, when I stilled his hand and purred, "We'll be needing that." He grinned wolfishly, and braced himself with his hands to lean over and claim my mouth again. I jerked his jeans open, and he sat up to remove them along with his underwear, as I shimmied out of my panties.

Now that he was naked, I got a good look at his penis, already hard, with glistening pre-come atop it. Wetting my lips, I met his eyes and sighed, "Make me do whatever you've been imagining."

Triumph spread across his face. He stood and commanded, "Kneel down here in front of me."

Joy filling me at the pleasure of being topped, I rolled off the bed and did as he told me. Flicking black strands of hair out of my eyes, I looked up at him and asked, "What do you want me to do?"

His hand snaked out to tangle in my hair, a sudden tender vulnerability crossing his visage, and he murmured, "Suck me, Leslie." Keeping my eyes locked to his the entire time, I leaned forward and rubbed my lips lightly across the head of his dick, the drop of liquid there slicking my tender mouth. Then I closed my eyes, wrapped my hand around the base of him, angling his dick downward, then swooped my mouth over it, shoving his length down my throat and bringing tears to my eyes as my gag reflex kicked in.

It was a glorious feeling. His cock throbbed and jerked in my mouth, and I opened my eyes to peer up at him. His head was thrown back, and both his hands now gripped my head, forcing me to maintain the rhythm. After several minutes of my sucking and licking, he fisted my hair and pulled my head back none too gently. He eyed me, catching his breath, and huffed out, "Get on the bed." I did as I was told, lying on my back.

He kneeled between my legs and drove them painfully apart.

He then slid one of his glorious hands down to spread me open. He consumed me with his eyes, then teasingly flicked one finger down my clit and opening. I moaned and writhed, the long-needed attention sending streamers of pleasure through me. He pinched my clit, causing my back to bow and a cry to escape me. Then he positioned himself above me, and bumped my opening with the tip of his dick.

Sighing out pleas for fulfillment, I reached down to try to pull his hips to me. He sat back up and collected both of my hands into one of his. "I'm not going to do it until I'm damn well ready," he said. Then he levered my hands over my head and pinned them there with one wide palm. The pressure on my wrists was beautiful, bringing heat to my face and my cunt. He positioned himself again above me, and I resumed my begging. He nuzzled his mouth down into my hair and nipped lightly at the nape of my neck.

I sucked in a breath and arched up, my breasts flattening against his chest. He pressed his tongue stiffly into my pulse, scattering my senses, then plunged his member into me swiftly. I shouted, "Sonny, fuck!" He was deep inside me and pressing his hips harder against me, digging deeper. Then he slowly began to draw out and pump in again. I moved my trembling hips in time with his as he nipped at my neck. As he bit down, a frenzied passion shook me.

His pounding quickened as he sensed the new level of my ardor. He lifted his head and reached with his free hand, never breaking rhythm, to find the belt. He abruptly pulled out of me, leaving me gasping with an aching void, and deftly flipped me over. I lifted my hips, and he slammed home into me again. I felt the swing as he raised his hand, then brought it down to slash my skin with the metal studs and leather of his belt.

The immediate heat of the pain made me cry out, mindless with pleasure. "Harder," I yelled, and he complied, sending another lash across my ass, this time with more force. I felt blood trickle down my skin as I gasped with gratification. I felt his hand reach down to smear the blood up over my hip and wet my breast. Oh, he was so good. He knew instinctually what I wanted.

He pinched my nipples unmercifully. His hips crashed into mine, urging his cock deeper and harder. The he did another of his cruel pulling out acts, and flipped me back over. He reached down by the bed to his pants and pulled out a pocket knife, flicking it open with an expert movement of his wrist. My breath caught in my throat, and my eyes closed in antici-pation of the arousing bite of the blade. He submerged himself in my wet heat again, and lowered the blade to my breast.

My breathing quickened and I cried out as the sharp sting slid across the outer side of my breast. "Yes, yes," I urged him on. He lowered his head to lap at the wound he'd created, and both our movements became desperate and less smooth. He raised his head and pressed his bloody lips to mine, and the orgasm swept through me at the taste of my vital fluid inside his mouth.

As my inner muscles tightened on him, he bucked and slammed himself into me, bruising my hips, the violent friction of my sheath bringing his climax to a head. He erupted within me. We both shook wildly, muscles trembling with culmina-tion, experiencing carnal gratification on a cellular level. As he gave one last penetrating prod, he collapsed atop me, easing our intimate kiss to a light brushing of crimson lips.

I lay panting as he lifted his head to capture my gaze. "That was..." he began, but was interrupted by the opening door.

"What is going on here?" Shauna cried shrilly, a look of horror on her face. Sonny quickly rolled off me, wiping blood from his mouth, and we pulled the covers over us.

The following scene was horrible. Shauna threatened to charge me with statutory rape, but Sonny retorted that he was of age and could sleep with whomever he wanted to legally, no matter if he was still in high school. Shauna then told me that she wanted me out of her house. She fled down the hall to call my parents. I began hastily pulling on clothes, as did Sonny. As I began gathering my things, Sonny stood in front of me and took me by the shoulders.

He said, "Leslie, please don't just leave. I can't just never see you again."

I laughed, almost hysterically. "Sonny, that's exactly what you have to do." Then he swept me into an embrace and found my mouth with another crushing kiss. I accepted the kiss for a moment, then pushed him away, and began flinging things into my still open suitcase. "Sonny, you are great. I haven't had sex like that, ever. But you are just a kid. Your mom is right, I shouldn't have done it."

He looked hurt and said, "Just don't ever regret it, Leslie, because I won't, and I won't ever forget you." Then he left the room. That was the last time I saw Sonny. I left Shauna's apartment as fast as I could and drove home to face the music. Turns out the music was a dirge. My family disowned me. My mother called me a whore, my dad wouldn't even look at me. "You'll never settle down," they told me.

That turned out to be true. I lived with some of my old buddies, and ended up fronting a band and meeting the most amazing man. And I never used the degree that caused my father so much grief. I never saw my parents again.

That afternoon with Sonny changed my life, in ways that were both horrible and wonderful. I can't regret it, and I'll never forget the feel of his body. No one will ever measure up to the erotic play of pain and delight he inflicted upon me so intuitively. Can you blame me?

BLOWJOB

Jessica Lennox

One of my favorite bumper stickers is the one that says: "Gay. Straight. They all want blowjobs." I hope this doesn't sound too crude, but I've had my fair share of cock. Whether it was made of flesh and blood, or silicone rubber; whether it belonged to a man, or was donned by a woman; in my experience, everyone loves a blowjob.

I proudly consider myself a sex kitten, and I make no excuses for being a woman who enjoys sex. When I see something I like, I go for it. I've engaged in many sexual trysts with thrilling ecstasy, and I've done things most people wouldn't even dare dream about. Naturally, enjoying this kind of freedom, I surround myself with people who have the same attitudes about sex and sexuality. Life is too short to be repressed, especially around your friends.

My circle of friends (aka "perverts") enjoys talking about sex. We find much delight in sharing stories and experiences, and often we attend sex and fetish parties, together or alone. If it's been done, I've seen it, and have probably participated in most of it. But for all my sexual experience, there is one thing I've never done—I've never been the one to "strap on." Yes, I've been on the receiving end many times, and I've enjoyed it immensely, but I've never been the "giver," I've always been the "receiver."

I must admit, strapping on didn't hold a lot of interest for me; in fact, I'd had a rather adverse reaction to it. I didn't spend a lot of time worrying about it, but it did come up in conversation every now and again amongst my crowd. I had the same reaction each time: no interest whatsoever. But somewhere down the line, after participating in many of these discussions, I found myself experiencing some degree of "cock envy." There was something so powerful about having a cock—stroking it, watching and feeling it get hard—that I sometimes wondered what that would feel like, and I found myself a bit envious. I *had* always longed to say the words "blow me" as a comeback and have it mean something.

One night, after dinner with the perverts, a discussion ensued on the topic of blowjobs. The topic was: do women really like giving blowjobs, and if so, what in particular do they like about it?

The answers were rather what I expected they would be: enjoyment in giving pleasure, a feeling of control, or doing it as an act of submission, et cetera. Of course, this isn't meant to be representative of all women; I know there are women out there who absolutely loathe giving head and will have nothing to do with it. But for my friends, it was right up there with being fucked while being spanked, or being in the middle of a threesome. It was all good.

I hadn't given much thought to why I liked giving blowjobs, I just knew I liked it, and it was difficult for me to think deeply (no pun intended) about the subject while listening to everyone else talk about it. But later that night, I had quiet time to myself, and I let myself explore my own answers and reasons—which were pretty much along the lines of the others'. Still later, I fantasized about giving a blowjob to a complete stranger. This wasn't anything new—I liked this fantasy and used it often while masturbating. But this time there was one big difference—I realized that my pleasure came from the viewpoint of the one getting the blowjob, not giving it.

This realization shocked me to my core. When I thought back on all the times I had fantasized about this act, I realized I had always focused on the receiver and their pleasure, not my own pleasure as the giver. This felt like a betrayal, considering my "adverse reaction" to the idea of strapping on.

With this new realization, I was now hyper-aware that every time I fantasized, I was connecting with the receiver in the fantasy, and no matter how I tried to connect with the giver, I kept slipping into the role of the recipient. Even though it was strange, I found myself curious about it. This seemed like a new door opening, and I wanted to walk through it. I allowed myself to drink it in, to explore my feelings about it, and this led to something new—a growing obsession with the idea of *getting* a blowjob.

I wasn't really sure how I was going to accomplish this, and if I really even wanted to go through with it, but the idea was

starting to take hold. I mulled it over and quickly discarded
the idea of asking a friend—that would be too creepy. No, it
would have to be more anonymous than that. A personal ad?
Nah, that would involve way too much energy and potential
drama.

I finally settled on the idea of an anonymous encounter at
the next Submit party—New York's best queer/lesbian/trans-
gender sex-and-play party. I'd been to Submit parties before,
so I knew what to expect. There would be plenty of available
players to choose from, and plenty of people okay with the
idea of giving a complete stranger, a femme, a blowjob.

The next party would take place in three weeks, so that gave
me plenty of time to either make a plan, or abandon the idea
all together.

By the time three weeks passed, I was ready to take the
plunge. I had purchased a leather harness and a seven-inch re-
alistic cock for the occasion. I'd shopped for adult toys plenty
of times, but up till now, when it came to cocks, they were never for me to wear, always for whomever I was playing with at
the time. Still, I already had in mind what I wanted, and found
it easily at my favorite queer retail store.

As I dressed that night for the party, I was a bundle of nerves.
I ripped one pair of stockings and had to toss them out. Luck-
ily I had another pair or I would have had to change my entire outfit. The stockings fit perfectly with the garter belt I had
chosen and would work well with the harness. I chose a short
skirt that, if I did find a play partner, would easily allow access
to the surprise hidden underneath.

I arrived at the club about an hour after the party had started. It was a nice venue, well decorated and dimly lit. There
was an entry way with a door person where the admittance

fee was paid, and beyond that, a nicely furnished social area, where one could sit on comfortable sofas and chairs and have a snack and soda.

Further on was where the real fun took place. There were several pieces of play equipment, ranging from padded horses to cages, tables, and leather swings. By the time I arrived, several people were already engaged in scenes of all sorts, and I scanned the crowd of onlookers to see if anyone immediately caught my interest.

I spotted a somewhat shy-looking, petite young girl watching another couple playing. Something about her energy caught my attention, and I made my way over to where she was standing. I stood just behind and to the right of her, so I could look at her, but not engage with her right away.

Her energy and body language were pure submissive, but she also appeared confident, and my mouth watered at the idea of having her on her knees sucking my cock. I moved forward and bumped up against her, the cock pressing into her hip. "Oh, I'm sorry. Excuse me," I said.

She turned toward me, smiled, then quickly lowered her gaze. *Mmm-hmm,* I thought, *I was right—a natural submissive.* I looked her over and didn't see anything to indicate that she belonged to someone else, but one never knows, so I asked, "Are you here with anyone?"

She smiled, her beautiful brown eyes twinkling, and answered, "No, I'm not."

"Do you belong to anyone, or are you free to play?"

"I'm free, as soon as the right person comes along."

"I see," I said, smiling. "And how will you know when the right person comes along?"

She paused for a moment, then said, "It's a feeling I get. If they do or say something that makes me tingle, then I know they're the right one."

I didn't know if I should take that as a challenge or an opportunity, so I took her hand and pressed it against the outline of my cock and said, "Does that make you tingle?"

The look of shock on her face was priceless. She slowly nodded then shivered. I took that as a yes, and led her to a small room near the back of the club.

The room wasn't private, but it was very dark, lit only by the dim light coming in through the doorway. There were a few other people in there, in various stages of activity, but for the most part it was empty.

I chose an unoccupied bench and sat down, motioning for her to sit beside me. She did, and faced me, keeping her eyes cast downward. I stroked her hair with my left hand, and held her hand in my lap with my right. She had this gorgeous, luxurious, long brown hair, and I loved the sensation of running my fingers through it. She began to relax and she closed her eyes as I continued stroking her hair. She looked beautiful, but I didn't want her to get too relaxed. I started tugging on her hair, gently, and she moaned. I stood up, and pulled her up by her hair. Her eyes opened then, but they were glassy and soft with desire.

I pulled her to face me, keeping one hand in her hair, and trailing the other over her lips and down her neck. I could hear her breathing getting faster, and when I trailed my fingers over her blouse and gently circled her nipples, she gasped. I continued to simultaneously tug on her hair, and stroke her nipples through her blouse. Her moans were getting louder, and I was so turned on, I almost couldn't stand it any longer. I forced myself to wait, just a few more minutes, while I continued to arouse her.

Finally, I couldn't take it. I pulled her hair in a downward motion, forcing her to her knees, keeping one of her hands in mine. She looked up at me, and I placed her hand on my skirt where she could feel the bulge of my cock. I forced her to rub it, to trace the outline of it, then I let go of her hand. She kept it there, not moving at first, but then she began to stroke it on her own. The pressure she was inadvertently applying to my clit felt great, but I wanted to see what her mouth could do.

I reached underneath my skirt and grabbed my cock, unveiling it. I stroked it slowly, in front of her face, an inch from her lips. I watched her watch me, as my hand caressed and squeezed it. This alone felt good, but I wanted more. I moved my hips forward and pressed the head of it against her mouth.

"I want to see your pretty little mouth around my cock." It was a command, not a request, and she complied by opening her mouth and taking the head in. The rush I felt was unbelievable. Watching her mouth suckle my cock was everything I had hoped it would be. She looked up at me and I smiled at her, letting her know this was exactly what I wanted. She continued to look into my eyes as she took more of it into her mouth, then started moving forward and backward, forcing the base of the cock against my clit. I was in ecstasy, and it was even better when she used her hand to squeeze it, while her mouth worked up and down the shaft.

I wanted it to last forever, but I was already on the verge of coming, and I started bucking my hips, forcing her to take more. It took just a few strokes, and I came hard, fucking her mouth and pulling on her hair for leverage.

When the throbbing in my pussy finally settled down, I sat back down on the bench, and pulled her up to sit next to me.

"That was amazing. Incredible even. Thank you so much. You have no idea how much I enjoyed it."

"Oh, I think I have an idea of how much," she said, smiling.

"So. Can we get together and do this again sometime?" I asked.

"Definitely. But how about next time, we switch places?"

My mouth gaped open, but then I realized it's true—everyone loves a blowjob.

THE BAD POET

Kay Jaybee

"You really are a terrible poet."

"You got my email then?"

"First thing this morning."

"And?"

"It was a very bad poem indeed, truly wicked."

"Got you here though, didn't it?"

"True. Although I am wondering if I should leave."

"And miss the opportunity to find out?"

"Find out?"

"How bad a poet I really am."

He'd lost count of how many times he'd read and reread her email throughout the day. He knew it by heart. She was right; curiosity had brought him to her flat. He replayed the poem in his head as they sat silent, on either side of her kitchen table, measuring each other up.

There are many things I long to do,
Tie you up before I screw.
Make you beg.
Make you whine.
Whip you till you scream you're mine.
Cover your flesh in lashes red,
Rope you tightly to the bed.
Force a howl.
Force a groan.
Watch you helpless; squirm and moan.
Make you lick me long and slow.
Watch you suffer as I glow.
Your lust ignored,
Your want denied,
Whilst my pleasure, you provide.
Perhaps I free you for a while?
Maybe touch you; make you smile.
Probably though,
I'll deny your need,
And just enjoy hearing you plead.

Confident that the poem would bring him here tonight, she had prepared carefully for his arrival. Black was the over-riding color. Black basque, black shiny boots, sheer black stockings. More importantly, black rope, black whip, and a black ball gag. His eyes scanned the objects she'd laid out on the table next to her, fully aware that she was waiting for him to react.

He was reacting; she probably knew he was, although she couldn't possibly have seen the growing bulge in his crotch from where she sat. His palms felt sticky as, once again, he ran through the poem's words in his head. Did she really want to do all that? To him?

Her eyes twinkled as she broke the silence. "You're wondering how I knew you'd come?"

"Yes."

"You have *servant* written all over you. I've studied these things." She ran the whip through her hands provocatively as she spoke, "Also, you were intrigued by the last verse; would I give you pleasure...or not?"

He shifted slightly and nodded in response. He could feel the balance of control tip in her direction as he watched her expert fingers manipulate the whip. In his mind he could already feel the sting.

The time to leave willingly with no coming back had passed. He was there, the lines of her strange poem running around his brain. It was, he thought as he watched her move toward him, almost an ironic piece. She rhymed like a child, but the words, the sentiment, the meaning was pure hurt, anger, danger, selfish desire. Yet he *was* here.

"Take off your jacket."

He did as he was told.

"And tie, shoes and socks."

Again he obeyed, heaping his garments onto the battered chair next to him.

"Shirt."

His fingers began to fumble as the tension between them rose. The lines *Make you beg. Make you whine* echoed around his head, as he stood meekly, his erection now obvious beneath his boxers.

She picked up her toys and ran the tip of the whip across his encased bulge, which leaped at the leather's touch, its head poked out between his waist band and his stomach. "Follow me." She turned and walked away.

He goggled at the view for a moment. The thong she wore accentuated her firm buttocks; the basque, tied so tightly, highlighted her slim waist and hips; and the impossibly high-heeled boots made him weak at the knees. He followed, every inch the submissive she had seen him to be. So far she'd done nothing, but he knew she was going to make him beg, and that knowledge, combined with the sight of her, was enough to stop him running for the door.

They entered a room dominated by a massive four-poster. His heartbeat quickened as she wordlessly pointed to it. He moved forward, more slowly now, until he stood between the end posts. She climbed onto the bed, and using the thin black rope, began to string up her willing prisoner, his hands as high up as they would stretch, his legs tied wide, starlike. Satisfied, she climbed down and, taking a pair of scissors from her dressing table, cut off his boxers with two precise surgical snips, making him flinch as the cold metal grazed his skin.

She was back on the satin cover now, arranging her toys in a pattern before him. The waiting was agony. She'd tied him up, and now, according to the poem, she was going to whip him until he begged her to stop. Why didn't she get on with it?

Taking her time, she turned to face him and, sitting tantalizingly close, undid the very top of her basque, pulling each lace slowly so that the roundness of her tanned breasts began to peek out of the top. His eyes bored into her as she freed each globe, passing the flat of her thumbs over the nipples. He could imagine how good her tits felt; he wanted to touch them, suck them. His cock strained toward her as she put a finger in her mouth and pumped it in and out of her reddened lips, causing him to flush all over with anticipation. Why didn't she just go on and punish him like the poem said? Even the pain would be better than having to watch her taunt him; having to wait.

She withdrew the wet finger and slid it down between her stretched-out legs, rubbing herself behind her thong until she sighed. Had he got it wrong? He ran the words through his head again. Of course. He had to beg first.

He didn't hesitate. "Mistress, please Mistress, take pity. Touch me, I beg you."

She smiled and withdrew her hand. He could see her fingertips glistening, she must be soaking. He marveled at her self-control as he watched her rummage beneath the pillows for something. It was a black leather cock case. He drew a sharp breath at the sight of the previously undeclared item. Quickly she enclosed his thick hard shaft. The case pinched against him, making him harder still. He didn't speak as she picked up the whip and moved behind him; he already knew what was going to happen next.

The whip trailed softly down his spine and the backs of his legs, beneath his aching arms and around each tight buttock before sweeping lightly over his balls, forcing a gasp from his dry mouth. She stopped and waited just long enough for him to wonder if she was still there, if she really was going to hit him, before aiming the first stroke across his back.

He screamed, winded by the strength behind the blow. Again, across his back, his legs, his arms, his arse. Again, and again and again. Tears sprang to his eyes as the burning sting coursed through him, his imprisoned cock leaping with each blow.

As she continued to create a pretty crisscross of red lashes against his skin, he began to burble, he wanted her to stop. He wanted her to kiss the wounds, lick him better, free him. His mind raced, he knew what to say, what was it? The pain was addling his brain. He forced himself to concentrate, flicking lines from the poem through his head.

"Mistress, I'll do whatever you want. Please stop. I beg you Madam. I'm yours, just stop."

The instant he uttered the words she dropped the whip to the floor and stood back to admire her handiwork. Red stripes covered his rear view, his head was drooped and his arms shook. He was hers.

Pausing for only a few more seconds she untied his legs and arms. He groaned as he flexed his limbs.

"On the bed. Back down." It wasn't a request.

He winced, fresh moisture gathering at the corners of his eyes as his burning back hit the cool satin sheets.

This time she just took his wrists and fastened them to some previously hidden black silk ties that hung from each side of the bed. He pulled at them, testing her work. He was held firm, helpless, but without the extreme discomfort of his previously stretched captivity. Now what?

She took off her wet thong and sat astride his chest. He could feel sticky juices smear against him as she got comfortable and began to undo the rest of her basque. Shrugging it off, she began to play with her tits again, rubbing them together before licking her fingers and circling them around her nipples. She started to groan at her own touching, moving her fingers faster, eyes closed, and her mouth mewling with pleasure, until finally she came. Her whole body shook against him, her quivers melting into his trapped body.

He whimpered hopelessly up at her, his eyes pleading, as she began again. This time she put three fingers between his lips. He gobbled at them gratefully. She laughed at his eagerness, before pulling them away and inserting them into her snatch, jamming them quickly in and out of herself, leaning back so that he could observe her working herself off.

Again she came, high on her own dominance, before returning her fingers to him to clean off with his tongue. He savored her taste, squirming beneath her, desperate for any relief, any movement which might bring his own satisfaction. This woman was insatiable.

His head swam as she sat on his face, continuing to fulfill her own selfish need. At least he could feel her properly now, and he became almost giddy at the scent of her sex as he darted his tongue across her clit. Then, remembering the poem, he began to lick her long and slowly, extracting a deep satisfied growl from her throat.

Seconds later she exploded against him, her third orgasm taking over as she rocked against his face.

As she rolled off him, leaving his mouth soaked in sweat and come, she watched his dick sway in its case. Little flecks of white pre-come dripped out of its sides. It was almost time. The poem was nearly over. Had he deserved pleasure, though?

She knew he wanted to speak, but he wisely remained silent. That was a point in his favor. He'd done well to stick to the poem's instructions. She made her decision, and carefully, so as not to provide additional stimulation, undid the cock case.

He failed to stifle his moan of relief as he felt air around his dick. He looked at her in hopeful expectation. Would she touch him? It was all he needed. Or would she still deny his need and just enjoy the sight of his suffering?

She leant close to him, stroking his hair, and whispered, "You are a very good boy," before kissing him hungrily. Her previous orgasms forgotten, she was ready to go again. He was too delicious to free. The sight of him trapped there, willing, delirious with craving for her touch, could keep her going all night.

He managed to stammer out, "Thank you, Mistress," his mouth dribbling. He didn't care. The final line of the poem ran through his mind. He knew what to do. He began to plead, his lips pouring out words of need, begging for her touch, making promises of future debasement and correction. Swearing eternal submissive devotion.

She swelled beneath his words. She said nothing, but nodded, and licking a single finger, lowered it very very slowly toward his cock. It seemed to take an eternity to travel from her mouth to his skin, but when it finally touched him he felt he'd been ripped asunder. Held by the silk restraints, his body jerked off the bed and his head swung from sign to side, as he screamed in relief.

"If you make a noise like that, then I'll have to use the gag." She picked up the whip again and stood by his heaving body. "So, am I a bad poet?"

He licked his lips, trying to form words from his dried-out throat. "You are a very bad poet, Mistress. I look forward to reading another of your pieces."

She trailed the leather across his chin. "I bet you do. Perhaps you could help me compose one?" She picked up the ball gag and, without waiting to hear if he objected or not, fastened it around his face. "No time like the present!"

FLOWERGIRL MEETS BOMB

msprism

She met her in the hotel lobby as requested, punctual to the second, easy to spot in that white retro Hanae Mori summer dress with the bold red hibiscus splashed across it. One leg was elegantly draped over the other as she delicately sipped her Armagnac; a white sandal dangled casually from her foot. She looked cool and relaxed in the afternoon heat.

Such a warm drink for a hot day, she thought, already overheated in her Moschino denims. Approaching quietly she observed the seated woman's features. Short dark hair, almost Latino black, shone in the soft sunlight; her features were regular and tanned, rather nondescript—the kind of face you'd swear you've seen a million times before in the street, a photo-fit of the blandest Caucasian features possible. It was certainly not eye-catching, but not unpleasant to look at either. The mouth had a fuller lower lip, and was painted to match the colors on the dress; the eyes were a fusion of the liqueur in the glass, honeyed caramel layered with a sensuous copper undertone, warm and rich, dancing with light; they were welcoming as they glanced up and looked directly at her.

The lips creased into a pleasant smile, revealing even white teeth. The woman set down the glass and rose to meet her, hand extended in a mannerly greeting.

"Flowergirl." She introduced herself as they shook hands. "How do you do?"

"Bomb." The handshake was warm, firm and inviting. "I'm well thank you."

Flowergirl gestured toward her glass. "May I get you a drink?"

"No thank you, I don't drink."

"Good. Let's go up to my room."

The room turned out to be a suite, understatedly elegant, like her. On entry she silently motioned Bomb to wait in the center of the lounge while she took a seat by the window.

"Tasya." The bedroom door opened and a diminutive young woman entered, dressed in a loose white linen top and trousers; her bare feet moved quickly and quietly across the thick carpet. Gracefully she flowed to her knees, as prim as any ballerina, head bowed before her Mistress.

"I'll have a soda water on ice with a twist of lime." The young girl floated to her feet and hurried away.

Flowergirl turned her attention to her guest. "You can disrobe."

As a cool breeze billowed the muslin curtains, she leaned

back into the soft upholstery and watched with idle interest.

Bomb bent and quickly removed her Havaianas sandals. Straightening to her full six foot two she removed the T-shirt next, freeing small sturdy breasts that pushed out from a honed chest and abs. The nipples puckered automatically. Next she unbuckled her belt, unzipped her fly and stepped out of her jeans; bending quickly from the waist she stripped off the black bikini briefs and stood almost to attention waiting patiently for inspection.

Tasya reappeared with the requested drink and, setting it on the coaster by her Mistress's elbow, once again sank onto her haunches, head lowered.

Ignoring the beverage and its bearer, Flowergirl sat for a few moments simply admiring the beautiful specimen before her. The tall Afro-American had turned quite a few heads as she strode confidently into the hotel foyer earlier. Broad shouldered, with shaven head, her fine facial features were feminine while her musculature provided an androgyny that was very attractive. Now, as she stood naked before Flowergirl, small breasted, mons shaved clean as requested, it was easy to admire the melding of skin tones from burnt toffee to bruised black across the topography of the woman's body.

Slowly rising, Flowergirl moved quietly toward the black woman standing motionless in the center of the penthouse lounge, her darkness contrasting vividly with the rich creams of the surrounding décor. Flowergirl was five foot five, but for her carriage and demeanor she may as well have been Everest. Passively she stood before Bomb and carefully ran her eyes over the body presented for her, noting every freckle and mole, regarding the dark areolas with lazy interest as they began to relax and take on the spongy texture of a flaccid nipple. She flicked her gaze over the tight abdominals, the furless mound and the sweep of strong thighs. All was in order, unflawed, unmarked and unpierced, healthy and vibrant. Slowly she strolled around behind the figure, silently admiring the massive latissimus dorsi and trapezius muscle groups, the high rounded buttocks and meaty hamstrings and calves. Finally she reached out one tapered finger, so pale and slender against the blunt back, and barely touching, traced the series of small glyphs tattooed from the nape of the neck down the top of the spine. There were three of them, each depicting a past Master or Mistress.

"Labarum," she murmured, grazing her nail along the Chi Rho cross initialing Bomb's first Italian Master. The skin goosefleshed under her fingertip, which pleased her; she liked sensitivity to her touch.

The next glyph was of a snake swallowing its own tail, "Ouroboros," she recognized again. Her finger trailed over the ridges of vertebrae.

"Ah," she sighed, "how I miss her."

The last was an ankh representing Bomb's time in the North of Africa. Again, no scars or man-made blemishes. She made one last sweeping gaze as she returned to face the tall woman. Pleased with what she had seen so far, she nevertheless kept her face emotionless.

Raising her arm she pointed to the open bedroom door in an unspoken command. Bomb moved toward the room, then stood just inside awaiting her next instruction.

"On the bed on all fours."

She did so, assuming the position with practiced ease, back straight, arms and thighs at a perfect ninety-degree angle, parallel to each other. She posed breathtakingly still, looking dead ahead, like a piece of mahogany furniture.

The first stroke of the riding crop came across the firmly fleshed orbs of her backside, absolutely level and center; the second was a few inches below that mean-line, the next above. A blink and the slightest sway at each blow betrayed the sting and shock to her system. The flesh heated and bloomed, red welts rose in crisp lines across the buttocks as more strokes filled in the three guidelines.

Less care for symmetry was given to the back of her thighs. This sensitive area brought a crinkle of a frown to the sheened brow. Several welts adorned her hamstrings before finally the crop was applied at random to her broad back. Here a myriad of criss-crosses patterned from shoulder to kidneys, every stroke being of equal strength to the last, every one raising a red echo of itself without breaking the skin. She never made a sound.

Resting, Flowergirl moved directly behind to view with pleasure the soaked sex protruding shyly toward her from between the apex of the chunky thighs, the shaven skin slick with excitement. She was aware that she too was wet in response to these sodden folds and the energy she had put into the flogging.

"Get up." Throwing away the crop she pointed to where she wanted Bomb to stand.

"Tasya." The Russian girl hurried into the room.

"Strip." White linen immediately pooled on the cream carpet.

"Bed." Tasya crawled onto the brocade cover just vacated by Bomb and assumed her kneeling position, sitting on her heels, palms on her knees, waiting.

Flowergirl now turned to Bomb. "Undress me."

Immediately stepping forward, Bomb moved behind the

smaller woman, lowered the zipper, and the dress spilled off her shoulders and over her naked breasts, which were full and rose tipped. Flowergirl carefully stepped out of the floating fabric and it was at once draped over a nearby chair. Turning, she kicked her sandals off, and standing with her back to the bed and Tasya, she waited as the tall woman knelt before her to gently draw the silk panties down her thighs and off her feet. She noticed the nostrils aligned with her sex quivering at her scent, and a small smile crept across her lips. This was correct behavior. All three women were motionless for a moment before she sat down on the edge of the bed.

"Cradle me," she cast over her shoulder. Shifting quickly to obey, the paler girl bodily cupped her Mistress, a thigh splayed either side of her as armrests, and back to belly the dark head cushioned against small round breasts. Bomb still knelt before the bed, level with Flowergirl's furred sex as she lay back on the younger woman.

"Touch me, Tasya." Small practiced fingers reached around her and began to knead her full breasts, circling the areolas with knowing pressure. Slowly Flowergirl opened her legs before the kneeling woman, never blinking as she watched deep brown eyes drink in her pink saturated sex.

She shifted slightly under the delightful ministrations of Tasya's skillful fingers; her nipples were fully erect, each tug pulling all the way through her core straight down to her cunt. She looked directly into the dark eyes hovering before her and said, "Eat me." Bomb's head bowed, her thick tongue burrowing even as the words were uttered. The pulsating heat from her striped back and buttocks poured from her mouth into the soft folds opening before her. It was an honor to feed on someone of the stature of Flowergirl. She speared as deeply as she could, rolling her tongue around the textured inner walls, tenderly grinding the outer lips against her teeth. Her hands remained on the floor before her to give balance as she gorged like a starving animal on a carcass. Only her mouth could touch until she was told otherwise. She angled her head slightly so her rounded nose nudged the stiffened clitoris pushing out to meet her.

The hands on Flowergirl's breasts stroked mercilessly, with firm teasing strokes she herself had taught the girl. Occasionally a small hand would cup a breast and gently nestle it in a cool palm before kneading the entire globe, and then return to the aching pink tips. Tasya was panting and Flowergirl knew the young slave's gaze was traveling down the length of her body to where the shining black head was tearing expertly into her. She could feel the girl's pebbled nipples scraping her shoulder blades. Her own eyes were feasting on the same sight; her hips began to grind back down onto the tongue and teeth below her, her own breathing rasping from her throat. She was thrashing now, heaving her ass up off the bed trying to make contact between her pulsing clit and the thick penetrating tongue that seemed intent on sucking her dry.

"Suck me," she managed to moan out of a tight throat. Bold lips immediately encircled her humming clitoris, drawing on it deeply, pulling and tugging on it, then releasing only to suckle gently. Tasya continued the generous kneading of both breasts, while the dark head between her legs rolled and swayed as Bomb ate her out. Her nails clawed across the Russian girl's milky thighs as she heaved herself into orgasm, crying out cradled in her slave's arms, sex opened to the gorging greed of her visitor.

When the sheen that coated her had dried, she rose up, barely glancing at the bleeding scratches on Tasya thighs, ignoring the bowed black head of the still kneeling figure.

"Tasya, help her clean up…run me my bath as well." They both stood and Bomb quietly followed the smaller woman to one of the bathrooms.

Alone now, Flowergirl lifted the phone and dialed a Cairo number. "I'm pleased. The money will be in your account tomorrow end of business." Replacing the handset, happy at the latest acquisition to her stable, she smiled and lit a French cigarette.

HER(HIS)STORY

K. L. Gillespie

Be careful what you wish for, so the saying goes. Well I always was, and I always wished for the same thing. For as long as I can remember, every birthday candle blown out, every shooting star in the sky, every coin thrown in the well was all about one thing.

I wished for it so hard one morning it came true....

Maybe the Gods heard and took pity on me. I can see them now, crowded around their crystal ball or whatever, scanning the earth for people's lives to play with. They must have been bored with the usual miracles of life, death and lottery wins, and when they saw me that day, wishbone in one hand, sprig of mistletoe in the other, they must have thought all their Christmases had come at once.

Maybe they'd been playing with me from the beginning, a cruel experiment conjured up for their own entertainment. I'm sure they do this a lot—you only have to look around you to see that. Why else would people be so screwed up? It's not the devil making work for idle hands, it's the Gods finalizing the lineup for their Holy Variety Performance; headlining tonight—Kim Nicholson (that's me by the way) and her all-consuming penis envy.

I've always wanted a cock. I suppose it's not that unusual, Sigmund Freud built a career out of labeling this need and analyzing it from every angle. According to silly old Sigmund this is quite normal, and when I reached adolescence I should have replaced my desire for a penis with the desire for a baby, specifically a baby boy with a penis—but this never happened. For me it was much more than just wanting to be a man and fit into a patriarchal society; it was an obsession that I just couldn't shake. I still wanted one when I was thirteen, fifteen, eighteen, twenty-nine.... I can't have children, by the way, and I've often wondered what Herr Freud would make of that.

There's a story my mum likes to tell every chance she gets; to her it's like showing new boyfriends photos of me in the bath when I was a baby, but to me it was the seed from which my whole obsession germinated. Oh! If only she knew. Anyway, Mum's favorite anecdote goes like this:

Mum: What do you want to be when you grow up?

Me: A daddy

Mum: Oh, honey, you CAN'T grow up to be a daddy. Daddy's have penises. You are a girl; girls have vaginas—not penises.

Me: I might grow a penis.

Mum: No sweetheart, you won't grow a penis.

Me: Well, girls grow boobies, why can't they grow penises?

Mum: True. When girls become women, they DO grow breasts. However, they DON'T grow penises.

Me: Then I'll BUY a penis!

And I did. By the time I was twenty-one I had a drawer full of multicolored dildos. I never did like being told there was something I couldn't have.

I've never been able to forge a lasting, loving relationship with any of my sex toys and I've never been able to forge a passionate, wanton relationship with my husband. (Oh, did I forget to mention I was married? His name is Mick and it's seven long years since the happy day.) Nevertheless, between my bottom drawer and my bottom-of-the-rung, bargain-bin husband I had most things I needed, but not everything, as the smooth sweep of my pudendum kept reminding me.

I would lie in the bath until the last bubble had melted, just imagining what it would feel like to fuck and be fucked at the same time and thrusting my fingers in and out of myself until the water splashed over the edges and soaked the tufted carpet.

When Mick and I first got married I would make him stand naked in front of the mirror and then position myself behind him so that my head rested on his shoulder. If I squinted I could block out his face and see only my own and his body became mine. I would reach around and take my cock in my hands and stroke it for hours. He wasn't allowed to speak or move; he didn't know why and he never asked, but it was the strictest rule and it had to be abided by or the illusion would be shattered.

Plato claimed that the original human was hermaphroditic. These two halves were sundered and cursed to go eternally in search of each other. Mick wasn't my other half; the cock I didn't have was.

Sex with Mick was usually strictly missionary and he was of the tender and loving school of thought that most men think women like. Oh, how wrong he was; I wanted it hard, fast, thrusting and violent. Throughout the whole drawn-out experience all I could think was that if I had a cock I'd show him how to fuck; I'd show him what to do with it. This thought started infiltrating my mind more and more and I became obsessed with the idea of sodomizing my husband.

I have always had a voracious sexual appetite, like a man! Mick calls me rapey after a few drinks and I know what he means.

Anyway I bought a strap-on from a mail-order company on the Internet. They didn't sell things like that in Buxton; we didn't even have an Ann Summers for god's sake. I didn't think Mick would mind; in fact, I would have bet my best handbag that he'd been secretly gagging for it. Most men are you know, even if admitting it is the last thing in the world they would do. They give to receive—it's in their nature. I know, I've seen it in their eyes when we're fucking. I've seen into the very depths of their souls. I've tasted their fantasies every time they come in my mouth.

I badgered him for months, subtly introducing the topic at first. I told him everyone did it, all the celebs loved it, footballers especially (he was a big Arsenal fan, still is).

Eventually he agreed to let me fuck him on a Friday night when we got home from the pub, but as soon as I'd strapped my rubber cock on it just made me more aware of my lack. I couldn't feel anything when I touched it and its glossy red sheen just reminded me how synthetic it was. Of course he flaunted his, rearing it up in front of my face as it pulsed with life.

Nevertheless, I went through the motions, carefully applying the synthetic lubricant to my synthetic cock. Mick kept his eyes closed while I prepared and he never said a word. As if he had transported his mind somewhere else, leaving only his body shell behind like I've read so many rape victims try to do when they are being violated. But this wasn't like that, was it? This was within a marriage where partners make concessions for each other's happiness.

I have to admit I was surprised how much resistance he put up, even after three bottles of wine. He must have been nervous. After all this was a new and wholly unexplored territory for him and I was more than aware of the stigmas attached. So I took it easy to begin with, but my patience soon began to wane and he looked so weak and pathetic bent over the bed that he made me want to hurt him, to punish him for having the thing I wanted most. So I steadied myself with my hands on his hips and with one solid swing I thrust my strap-on deep inside his arse.

He cried out loud, from shock more than anything else, but within seconds my dirty little whore was enjoying it. He moaned and groaned in a cheap pastiche of the noises I made when he fucked me, a copy of an imitation—oh, the irony.

There was no money shot, no earth-shaking moments, no sticky mess to clean up afterward. I just ran my strap-on under the tap in the bathroom and we went to bed without looking at each other or saying a word. Him from guilt, me from disappointment.

While he slept I lay in bed, silently crying, mourning my lack, cursing Freud for labeling it, and wishing until my head hurt that my sorrow might be rectified.

That night I had the strangest dream, all in grainy black-and-white, as if I was watching a film. In the dream I was heavily pregnant. It was so real I felt the muscles in my back straining from the extra cargo in my swollen belly. My waters broke and I went into labor, alone on the bathroom floor in a pool of my own liquid. The pain was excruciating and I pushed and pushed like my life depended on it. Suddenly the pain stopped and I looked down to find a perfectly proportioned penis, complete with balls, the size of a newborn baby, lying in a pool of afterbirth.

Then I woke up.

I thought no more about it, as you tend to do with most dreams that don't involve the death of a loved one, and got on with the morning as usual.

That afternoon I was masturbating in the bath when I noticed my clitoris was bigger than usual. To begin with I just thought it was swollen from all the rubbing, but the next day it was still peeping out from my labia and it had a foreskin. If I'm honest, I have to say that I knew what it was as soon as I saw it. I wasn't even particularly shocked. It was almost as if I had spent half my life expecting it, waiting for it to appear.

I stayed in the bath for hours, caressing my new appendage, hardly believing my luck. I wanted to phone my mother and tell her she had been wrong; I did have a cock; my very own, perfectly formed penis, just like I told her I would one day.

I've always believed that gender was just a linguistic construction, another pigeonhole to keep people in their places. Of course my beliefs were thwarted by the physical practicalities—until now. Isn't it every man's fantasy to have his own breasts to caress while he jacks off? Here I was living my version of that fantasy. I felt so powerful, so complete.

Hermaphrodites have always fascinated me; they're so exotic, otherwise, magical, everything rolled into one—and now *I* was one.

Within a week, if I stood naked in front of the mirror with my legs apart I could see it dangling between my thighs, and it just kept on growing. Within a month it was five inches long, and yes, of course I measured it, wouldn't you?

On the ninth day I had my first erection. I was driving into town, listening to the radio when the song that I lost my virginity to came on. Well, you know how music triggers memories and before I knew what was happening my cock was pressing against my jeans as the blood rushed from my head into it. I was so proud, like new parents when their baby smiles for the first time or gurgles its first word.

I pulled over into a rest stop and unzipped my trousers. I knew the Gods would be watching and to thank them for the gift I decided to give them one hell of a show.

To begin with all I could do was look at it, straining its neck toward the sun, vibrating with life and begging to be touched. Who was I to refuse?

I explored every square inch of it, reveling in its pulsating beauty, just feeling the fullness of it all between my fingers. I ran my fingertips slowly up one side and back down the other, shuddering at the otherworldly intensity of it all. I teased the most sensitive areas, swirling my thumb gently over my glans, my corona, my cock. I twisted the foreskin gently and cried out in unforeseen ecstasy. I felt things I hadn't imagined in my wildest and most hopeful fantasies and of course I thanked the Gods. Oh god, did I thank the Gods....

Suddenly I caught sight of my face in the side mirror, flushed and on the verge of ecstasy. I was so happy, so proud—I wanted every car that passed to see, every driver to pull in and witness the miracle I was experiencing. I adjusted the rearview mirror so that I could watch myself from another angle and then an idea hit me. I slid my pants down and while one hand was thrusting the skin of my penis back and forth I slid the fingers of the other into my slit. It sucked them in, desperate for some attention, and I reveled in the fact that I was experiencing the ultimate wank, and fuck me, it felt good, too good, and within minutes both my sexes had climaxed in unison. I laughed to myself as my cock wilted and my vagina constricted. I felt whole, on top of the world and apart from the world at the same time. I was the luckiest woman alive and as I tucked myself away and readjusted the rearview mirror I felt like I had only just become my true self.

From then on I masturbated every chance I got. I wanked myself raw with both hands for the first few days; who wouldn't if they could frig with one hand and jerk off with the other?

I even jacked off in the toilet at the supermarket. As soon as the thought crossed my mind I knew there was no point fighting it, so I abandoned my cart in the frozen food aisle and half walked, half ran to the ladies' loo.

I surprised myself with the things that made it grow. Oh, there were the usual suspects: the boy in the dry cleaners—pert arse, tight trousers; memories of trysts long gone with men that weren't my husband; my best friend's husband; and Johnny Depp, of course. But some of the other things surprised me: women's thongs peeping over trousers and the thought of where that string went, my own breasts, porn film clichés. Sometimes I thought I was turning into a man but I went with it. I felt like a pioneer and I didn't want to miss a second of this experience.

I even bought a porn mag from the newsstand, completely without shame even when I had to ask the assistant to get it down from the top shelf for me because I couldn't reach. The cheeky scamp asked me if I was a lesbian and I smiled sweetly and told him I was much more than that. He didn't say anything but I could see in his eyes that he wanted to know more. I paid for the magazine and left him wanting.

I couldn't get over the novelty of wanking, but I was desperate to fuck myself too and as soon as my penis was long enough I bought a bottle of wine, slipped into something flimsy, lit some candles and set about seducing myself.

Gore Vidal once joked that the advantage of bisexuality was that it doubled your chances of a date on a Saturday night. Well, I now had the third option of a good night in on my own. Mick was on a stag night and I knew he wouldn't be home until the early hours, so I drank the wine and began.

I bent my most prized possession back on itself and threaded it inside. I could feel it growing, as the blood rushed from my head and its head gently nudged at my slick opening.

Zeus posed a question thousands of years ago that has been puzzling man (and woman) kind ever since—is sex better for a man or a woman? I was about to find out and I couldn't wait.

If I'm honest, it was disappointing, frustrating even; the mechanics just weren't working, but it whet my appetite for fucking and I waited in the dark for Mick to come home, like a black widow spider.

He stumbled in three sheets to the wind at about half past two in the morning and I was ready and waiting. I helped him into bed, undressed him, and he was grateful, thought I was the adoring wife, concerned for his well-being. He had no idea. He was drifting in and out of sleep as I turned him over.

He tried to kiss me but I dodged his mouth, this wasn't about love, this wasn't about him—this was about me. I didn't seduce him; I didn't have the patience, my cock was burning and he felt so cold. Zeus wasn't going to have to wait much longer for his answer.

As I nudged his opening he mumbled something along the lines of "Oh no, not this again"—and made a feeble joke about not being able to sit down for a week after last time. I whispered in his ear that it was different this time and I shifted upward to let him feel my throbbing erection with his mouth. He tasted me and he liked it; his inhibitions were down and I made the most of it. I told him I was going to show him what fucking was about and I did. I fucked his arse until he was crying out for mercy and even then I didn't stop. I fucked and I fucked until I thought my head would explode and he loved every second of it. I felt born again.

Of course in the morning Mick couldn't handle it. A wife with a bigger package than him, what would his mates in the pub say? He felt dirty, he felt violated. He couldn't see me as a woman anymore. I was a freak in his eyes and the thing that upset him the most was the pride I took in it all. He decided to leave that morning and I haven't seen him since, although I've heard rumors that he's shacked up with his best mate, the stag, who called the wedding off the night before walking down the aisle. I hope he's happy—I know I am.

Now I'm just like all the other complex things in the world that are neither one thing or the other. I want to know everything, I want to be everywhere and I want to fuck everyone in the world. And I will.

THE LONELY ONANISTA

EllaRegina

In its original incarnation "The Lonely Onanista" was a Craigslist personal ad under Casual Encounters—one of eleven posted anonymously over a six-month period. Initially proper ads, they morphed into "vignettes" and ultimately became full-fledged stories. This ad— ninth in the series—was voted into the "Best-of-Craigslist" archive.

I am living inside the Washington Square Arch. There are no windows so it's a bit tomblike and claustrophobic, although a rudimentary air circulation system is provided through the nostrils and buttonholes in the façade's marble statues. On the rare occasion that I need oxygen I seek the great outdoors—I egress and enter through a secret hatch in the left-hand pocket of George Washington's breeches, something not patently obvious to the unwitting onlooker.

I have been hired by the Department of Parks and Recreation to do an interior décor project that entails completely wallpapering the vertical surfaces in dollar bills and paving the entire floor with quarters, edge to edge. I lodge in a tiny spartan room at the top, reachable via a cast iron spiral staircase, where I sleep beneath a pane of glass in the roof (the structure's only source of natural light) on a single-sized Army-style metal cot, under an itchy woolen blanket. Other accoutrements: a sink, toilet and bidet. I've also been supplied with a hotplate and a small refrigerator but I don't do much cooking, preferring instead to rely on Balance Bars, Urban Park Rangers' semen and the occasional falafel takeout from my favorite place on Mac-Dougal Street as sustenance.

My work is painstaking and requires many breaks. I fill this time by reading, writing, masturbating, and entertaining the various Park Rangers whose job details also necessitate frequent pauses. They all have keys and enter the Monument the conventional way, through a door on the Arch's western side, scaled for a child's playhouse. They must stoop while entering, an amusing picture, especially given those hats they wear. I never know who might show up or when and this unpredictability gives my long days some excitement. And while their visits are indeed fun I am tiring of the Park Rangers—they each would like to plant their seed and grow little trees inside my belly but I will have none of it. I have no time to tend nurseries and have told them so. I put in a request with Human Resources to be allowed outside "entertainment assistance"—

beyond the roster of Park personnel—and it has been approved.

You will be sent a rudimentary map of Washington Square Park, where a red circle indicates the location of a certain elm tree with a knot containing a key to the Arch door, hidden for you in plain sight, Boo Radley–style. You will enter the Monument and climb the black staircase. You will find me in my little garret, on my stomach atop the narrow bed, naked except for a pair of black kitten-heeled boots that end at midcalf. My legs are wide apart, spreading myself open—I've hooked the boots into the corners of the bed's metal footboard—except my knees are slightly pointed inward like pigeon toes so you have a mostly unobstructed view of the goings-on, what little there is to see.

I am masturbating, both hands at the ready underneath me, arms akimbo. This is my preferred position. My ass is gently bobbing up and down at a quick even pace, somewhere between allegro and presto, if I were a metronome. My body is completely taut, like a rope in a tug of war game played by Marines, every sinewy muscle in my legs, arms, shoulders and back well defined and twitching as a result of my efforts. My buttocks clench, right and left, involuntarily, occasionally revealing a spasm, my molars grind and chatter as if I were shivering. An extremely sensitive clitoris dictates the need to have a layer of material between fingers and body. Thin cotton handkerchiefs suffice and one is in place—I'm lucky to have found a vintage store nearby with a seemingly unending supply. My favorite Ranger, the one with the sense of humor, has already visited me today and before leaving has dropped a load of quarters, stacked within a tied condom, inside my rectum, as ballast. A very thoughtful gesture, considering the fact that my complex yet simple Onanistic process involves using my body weight/gravity in combination with the pressure from my fingers beneath me to cause the pleasure I seek. It's basic physics, really. The O end of the coin-packed condom sloppily protrudes from my anus in a clown's grimace.

You approach the left side of the bed, the direction where my head is turned. My face is at its edge—I am in a somewhat diagonal pose—and I look up at you, my dark hair in disarray, fallen over my pale face, my bangs in choppy clumps across my forehead. You see one big brown eye following your gaze, half a nose, a portion of mouth, its carmine lips slightly parted. You are still fully clothed. You unbutton your coat and take it off along with your beret and scarf. I watch as you undo your pants, slowly, button by button. I would reach out and admire the soft wide-wale fabric of the corduroy but my hands are totally occupied. You extract your prick from its hiding spot. It is fat and long and I can see that it is already slightly throbbing. Although it is not the optimum setup for such things, given your height and the relative counterpoint of my horizontal state, you introduce yourself, in lieu of a handshake—another formality not physically possible at the moment—by gently easing your warm erection into my eager mouth, the saliva there already welling, and yet despite the awkwardness of our respective postures it is a most pleasant how-do-you-do. But, oh, I would so very much like to be able to properly arrange myself around your sweet upright cock and give it the salutation it so richly deserves!

You take off your shirt, your undershirt. I ask you to keep your pants on as well as your shoes. You get onto the bed and between my legs, move my knees apart and sample, with your fingers and mouth, the glistening egg white substance emanating from my body. You lay yourself on top of me, facedown, your body perfectly aligned with mine, like open scissors. Your corduroy on my nakedness, your shoes decisively holding my booted feet still, your heavy knockwurst—now steadily pulsating—in repose along the length of my ass crack, cradled as if in a warm bun. I am aware of your heart pounding, almost in unison with my metronome beat. I match my breathing to yours. You lightly bite the nape of my neck, tug my head by the hair, then release it. Your belt buckle presses into the small of my back, hurting me, and I suggest that you remove it. You pull the leather strap from your pant loops in one motion, like an expert swordsman removing his rapier from its scabbard, and throw it to the floor. My ass is tilted slightly upward, giving the hands below me room for leverage. This stance offers you the perfect angle for your entrée. You guide your prick inside me, slowly but firmly, filling me up. You lie there for a few moments, not moving, keeping enough stress on my body to make me feel in your command yet allowing me space to freely continue pleasuring myself.

You begin to thrust, at first exactly corresponding to my speed but soon I find that I am following the tempo of your movements instead of leading with my own. The roll of coins imbedded in my ass puts some weight on your prick and this excites you. You grind into me, con gusto, gradually increasing the intensity of your delivery. At a certain point I use all the energy I can muster, untangle myself from your powerful restraint and draw my legs shut. I hold them rigidly, as if they were glued from cunt to heels, knees pressed immutably together. I like doing this. It makes your plunging more challenging yet you are of such sufficient length that you don't dislodge a millimeter—there is a sensation of unretractable tightness, as if you were fucking the virgin of all virgins. I squeeze my buttocks, amplifying the effect.

The original idea was that you would "assist" me. I am, in the end, an Onanista, generally used to pleasuring myself, thanks to the lonely confines of my profession. But you have other plans. You use the strength of your own muscular knees, thighs and feet to break open my tight wishbone of a leg grip. You get on your knees, encircle my small waist with your hands and draw me up to a kneeling position, ass in the air, head down. I look to the side and see dozens of George Washington's eyes staring back at me. You release your grasp of my midsection and grab my hands from under me. They were still in their repetitive fingertip-tapping, trying to get myself where I needed to go. But you will not let me. You announce that my training wheel days are over and that I have to learn how to ride without them now. You confiscate my handkerchief—the ultimate taunt—put it to your nose, inhaling its luscious scent, and then shove it into the pocket of your corduroys. Your pants have been half on and half off until this point. Now you fiercely kick them down, but not off, exposing your nakedness. You take my arms by the wrists and hold them together against my back. You resume your activity, flesh to bare flesh this time. My face is no longer in view and has practically embossed its features onto the sheet like the Turin Shroud due to your force. All that can be seen of my body on the bed is a round mountain of ass—with its narrow peak of waist—atop a tri-angle of open legs, hip to knee, my arms held behind me, your prick a blur of motion going in and out of my pussy.

You know what you are doing. I can sense that the finish line is just around the bend—"Look, Ma, no hands!"—and I sense that you sense it too, and that you are neck and neck with me in the race. You push harder into me, with such vigor that my body actually moves to the head of the bed. Were it not for the wall to stop me I would be doing a full somersault onto the floor. You can hear my teeth knocking again—my lower jaw swinging uncontrollably from side to side—a sure signal that the end is near. You are encouraged by that, the fruit of your labor, tangible proof that you are having a major effect on me, and it propels you wildly and then, suddenly, it starts—con-vulsing together: pussy, ass, prick. Feral sounds are emitted. You feel the coins in my ass moving from side to side in my everything jiggle. If they weren't so tightly packed they would be ka-chinking a tune like a pocketful of loose change. You let yourself go and lay some nice hot eggs deep within me, not stopping until your balls are completely empty.

We rest, you slumped on top of me, moist with sweat, yours and mine; your pants at your ankles, your arms around me, cupping my small breasts, one in each hand. Our heartbeats gradually return to somewhere between larghetto and adagio and slowly you begin to collect yourself and your belongings. I, too, have things to do and places to go. I throw on a long velvet dress and a black coat and see you down the staircase to the too-small door. We emerge from the Arch into the dark-ness of the Park. The Rangers have gone home for the night, their empty Flintmobiles lined up in a silent row. I let you keep the key. We part. You walk eastward with a fragrant souvenir in your back pants pocket. I walk in the opposite direction toward Sixth Avenue—your runny eggs making shiny lines down the insides of my thighs, knees, calves; the stack of coins a stiff reminder in my ass—and head off in search of more handkerchiefs, just in case you never return.

LOST AT SEA

Peony

Has it been that long? The clocks and the calendars are conspiring once again. Surely not? Have I been wandering, trapped in this haze, paralyzed by the thought of you? What day is it?

I shuffle to the bathroom amidst the chaos of the house. Things don't seem to be where I left them, nor do they seem to be the same. Nothing seems to be sane either, anymore. My reflection in the mirror stares back at me with shiny glass eyes. I am no longer seeing through these strange holes in my head and navigate mothlike and by memory, hearing and feeling for the last traces of you.

Showering mechanically, I scrape at my skin and the nest of my hair. The hot water trickles out and turns cold. I stand there as my rubber flesh changes from pink to white, and my veins shrink from the surface and nestle closer to my bones. I suppose it must be very cold, for my skin is prickled and protesting. I hazily ponder the idea that my brain might have severed its ties to my body and is bobbing listlessly, without anchor, in the sea of my skull. I used to hate cold showers.

Of their own volition my feet find their way to the bath mat, my hands to the towel and I'm rubbing robotically. I'm temporarily distracted by the absurdity of my joints sticking out at peculiar angles. Was I always this disjointed and bony?

Emerging from the bathroom I survey the damage. The house is littered with remnants edged with the feeling of emptiness, like a fairground after the circus has left town. Even the sound of my exhalations is loud in comparison and swells out into the room in ragged clouds. My leaden feet slide onto the shards of the glass long since shattered; I suppose it must be somewhere, somewhere down there.

I wonder how long I stood there, naked in the midst of the aftermath, blood collecting under my toes, staring blankly at the enormous hole in the shell of this decaying house. It loomed large and imposing, a porthole to another dimension, the name hanging rustily on hinges holed in my head. It's a door. The front door.

I stopped trying to make sense of it and decided to surrender. If I just give in, maybe I'll find a way out. There's no sense in fighting an irrepressible tide. Perhaps I'm walking in circles following reddened footsteps on floorboards that will probably never end.

You. A synapse fires inside my head. Somewhere near the surface I can see a faint glow fractured by surface ripples. I must be a long way under. We shouldn't have. We did. It's done and cannot be undone. We're on the other side of that which had grown so large between us, the lust that devoured us, swelled fat from the absurdity of it.

You again. Brighter now, refracting like strewn crystals from an exploded chandelier. You. The thought of you burns into a focal point with a brightness that is piercing. I'm rapidly ascending with no time to adjust, chest contorted from the pressure as I struggle to acclimatize. There is a roar in my ears as I rocket to the surface in an explosion of gray water and torn foam.

You again. I am awkwardly floating as I suck air through the cracks in my clenched teeth. I'm suddenly painfully aware of the dimension of space beneath and around me; it is terrifying being without the comfort of corners and walls.

You did this to me. With your hands that carved channels in my skin as you twisted my limbs to your pleasing and fed the burning inside me with pieces of you. You did this with words that pierced my insides with hooks that pinned me open, splayed and inviting, all yours for the taking. And yes, you took all of it, what I gave and what I didn't, you took it all and left me nothing save the taste of your skin and the weight of my heart in my hands.

I let you do this to me. At first we'd adhered to the rules and the rituals. The long lingering contact and words loaded and coated, then sitting so close you could smell the reek of the need burning under my skin. You'd played a deft hand and forced me to spread all that I held, face up and exposed. There is nothing more dangerous than one with none left to lose and though you might have won, being defeated was sweetened by the sound of my name on your tongue.

I'd read the words in your eyes and the space between lines

as I took my last look at the shore before diving headfirst. It was with such little tenderness that you pushed me beneath you and spread my limbs with your hands. These weren't lover's lips that stretched tight to expose my teeth that sank deep in your skin.

The pace was frenetic, fueled by the burning and the wheels sprung loose in my mind. There was no turning back or slowing the rhythm of the pounding both within and outside of my head. Skin flayed and breath burnt from the anger inside us, there is little to exchange when conquest leaves bodies ravished and broken. I had known it would be like this. I had hungered for the taste of it, flesh throbbing with the want of it, the want of you, to be taken, submerged, and surrounded, drowned and destroyed.

You were relentless and I was remorseless, for a time, just a short time, and then.

And then, it was over.

Laid beside without touching, silent and spent, I'm facing away from the fact of your face, from the sight of the redness of my nails on your skin. You've turned from the image that's too much like another's, the other, another, the one I was not.

REAR WINDOW

Scarlett French

Maria paid the guy and shut the door to her new apartment with a sigh of exhaustion. Leaning against a pile of boxes, she cast her eyes over the small flat, and considered the unpacking ahead of her. She threw open the huge sash window and put her head out to feel the breeze on her face. The air was warm and let up very faint smells of salt beef and garlic. The sounds of cars and horns below, and the wafts of the delicatessen, somehow made her feel that the city was welcoming her. Maria found excitement rising in her belly at the thought of this new beginning. She turned to face the unboxing of her life.

After a couple of hours of emptying boxes in no particular order, newspaper and bubble wrap flying, she realized it was growing dark.

Deciding it was time to call it a night, she grabbed one of the glasses she'd unwrapped, rinsed off the smudges of newsprint, and loped through to the living room. She found the bottle of wine she'd bought to celebrate her first night in the new place, and flopped down in her huge overstuffed swivel chair, right by the floor-length window.

The merlot was full-bodied and rich and she took long sips, letting it hit her taste buds before swallowing slowly. Finally relaxing, she leaned back into the chair and put her feet up on the windowsill. The cooler night air flowed in, replacing the balmy stuffiness of the day. The sun had gone down now but she made no move to get up and switch on a lamp: with the lights out she could keep her curtains open and still have privacy. It was a perfect way to explore her new view. She lit a cigarette and inhaled deeply. The smoke whipped out the open window and curled off into the night.

Hers was a typical high-rise view: an equally tall block opposite, lights from windows dotting the monolith in an irregular checkerboard pattern. As usual, there were the curtained windows—the muted squares on the board—and the brightly lit open windows of the people who didn't seem to mind that their lives were on display to at least ten flats in the building opposite. The view from their building would be a similar configuration. Maria sat cloaked in her big comfy chair, one of the black squares. She took a sip of the velvety merlot and dragged on her cigarette. There was something daring about watching other people's windows.

Directly opposite was a very white bedroom with its curtains wide open. It had the look of a showroom bedroom in an interiors store—white walls, white furniture, puffy white duvet and pillows. As she scanned the other windows, Maria suddenly caught movement out of the corner of her eye. She followed it back to the white room to find two men kissing in the doorway. Either they didn't realize that the curtains were open or they didn't care, because they made no move to draw them. Her first response was to look away from this private scene, but she found herself drawn in. Maybe just for a moment, she thought.

They were maybe in their midthirties. One of the men was very toned and had dark hair. He wore tight jeans and a black top and was rather perfect in his appearance, like a Calvin Klein model. The other was much less preened, in faded jeans and a plaid shirt. It was obvious to Maria that it was the Calvin guy's flat. Maybe Calvin liked a bit of cowboy rough? Calvin peeled his T-shirt off like a second skin while the cowboy wrenched open the snaps of his western shirt, letting it fall to the floor. Maria could see what the deal was here—these two men probably didn't know each other very well, and they wanted it. Bad.

With both their shirts off now, they immediately grabbed one another, their kisses forceful, their tongues sparring. The cowboy clutched Calvin's arsecheeks with both hands and pulled him in tight, pelvis to pelvis. Calvin began to kiss the cowboy's face and neck, working his way down to his nipples where he settled for a while. Maria saw the cowboy throw his head back in response to the teasing of Calvin's tongue. She also saw now the hard bulges in both of their jeans, and silently urged the two men to release them. Calvin continued his way down the cowboy's body until he reached the waistband. He licked his way along the cowboy's stomach, just above the belt, as he rubbed at the bulge in his own jeans. Maria heard an exhalation of breath and realized that it was her own. Her cigarette had burned down to the butt and the ash was sagging, about to fall away. Her glass was tilted, moments from spilling. She also realized she was getting wet. Collecting herself, she stubbed out her cigarette, then drained her glass and put it on the floor.

When she looked up again, she found Calvin tonguing the cowboy's crotch through the denim and attempting to unbuckle his worn leather belt. Words were exchanged and Calvin got up and pulled down his jeans and underwear in one quick movement. His stiff cock sprang out as he pulled them down past his thighs. Maria was suddenly self-conscious. What if they saw her? She slunk down a little in the chair and scooted it back into the shadows, just beyond the light of the streetlamps.

Calvin stepped out of his trousers and underwear and kicked them aside, then stood before the cowboy, waiting. The cowboy curled his fingers around his belt buckle and pulled hard. The belt flew through the loops and leapt into the air. Maria felt her clit twitch. She knew the sound the belt would have made, cracking in the air. She wanted to touch herself but held off in favor of keeping her full attention on the two men. Her pussy throbbed as the thrashing began. Supporting himself on a set of drawers, Calvin was bent over, proffering his arse to the cowboy. The folded belt came down hard on Calvin's bare skin and he jolted as the leather bit his flesh. His hard cock extended away from his body, twitching in expectation between blows. Even from a distance, Maria could see that Calvin's arsecheeks were reddening with each strike, showing welts of pleasure. There was something about the way the cowboy stood, legs firmly planted on the ground as he administered the belt, that triggered memories of some of the more butch lovers she'd had. Her cunt twitched and flexed, demanding attention.

When the cowboy decided that Calvin had been strapped enough, he flung the belt aside and pulled Calvin's striped arse toward his still be-denimed crotch, where he held him in place with muscled arms, thrusting and rubbing in Calvin's crack. Maria was sure she could see pre-come shining on the end of Calvin's cock. The cowboy dropped to his knees and began to lick Calvin's cheeks and inner thighs. Calvin spread his legs further, bending right over and raising his arse up. Maria could see his balls from behind—something the cowboy hadn't missed either—and watched as he took them in his mouth. Calvin's face fell into a gasp and his body writhed. Maria wished that she could hear the cries of pleasure, but settled instead on the sound of her own breathing, which grew heavier still.

Calvin turned and faced the cowboy, who devoured his throbbing cock immediately. Maria watched as the cowboy took it all in, all the way down to the base and back up again, leaving the shaft glistening with saliva. His head bobbed back and forth as he knelt, working Calvin's dick with fast, sure strokes. Calvin began to thrust back, fucking the cowboy's mouth. Maria was mesmerized; watching the cowboy, who clearly couldn't get enough meat, made her mouth water. The sheer desire between them was electric and Maria felt herself drawn in, willing Calvin to come. The cowboy grasped Calvin's arse, pulling him forcefully into his mouth, his lips sealed around his target. Calvin was panting and crying out something when he suddenly threw his head back and closed his eyes as his pelvis began to spasm on the cowboy's mouth. The cowboy gulped and swallowed, his Adam's apple moving in time with the spurts of Calvin's come. Maria's cunt clenched and throbbed, so she shut her legs for a moment to calm herself. *Watching is one thing*, she thought. As Calvin's orgasm began to slow, the cowboy pulled his face away and Maria saw a droplet of come shining in the corner of his mouth. He made sure Calvin was watching as he licked his lips greedily and smiled. In the apartment above, an old woman stood at her kitchen sink, moving her arms to place sudsy patterned china onto a dish drainer.

The cowboy rose to his feet and they began to kiss and shuffle backward toward the bed. Calvin finally pushed the cowboy who fell back onto the bed then looked up at Calvin, smirking. Calvin leapt on him and pulled roughly at his jeans, finally wrenching them off. To Calvin's obvious delight, the cowboy wore no underwear. His cock stood up proudly, uncut, and Calvin took it firmly in his hand and stroked it admiringly before straddling the cowboy. They kissed and clawed at each other as Calvin's cock, stiff again, banged against the cowboy's. Calvin licked the cowboy's whole body, progressively giving him a tongue bath. When he reached the cowboy's cock, he hesitated. It seemed that he had a tease planned, but he couldn't help himself—he gulped the cowboy's rod and gave it several luxurious mouth strokes that sent the cowboy arching backward. Despite herself, Maria found her hand had slipped into her underwear and was stroking away at her now rock-hard and very slippery clit. She didn't care anymore. Her pussy was engorged and every finger-slide through and up to her clit sent shivers coursing through her whole body. She paced herself; she wanted to come with the cowboy.

Still on the bed, Calvin directed the cowboy to get on his hands and knees and then got behind him. Leaning into him, he reached around for a while, sliding his hand up and down the stiff shaft, his own cock pressed hard between the cowboy's cheeks. He dropped back finally and pushed the cowboy's legs further apart. The cowboy's arse was slightly hairy and Calvin smoothed the hair down with broad tongue licks before spreading his arsecheeks wide. Making his tongue a point, he began to tickle at the cowboy's arsehole. The mirror beside the bed reflected the cowboy's eyes as they flickered closed and his facial expression became one of beatific pleasure. Maria could see that both of their cocks were throbbing as Calvin rimmed the cowboy with enthusiasm, licking and tonguing his puckered hole.

Maria watched mesmerized as Calvin rolled on a condom, then added lube and slid his dick up between the cowboy's spread arsecheeks. Holding it at the base, he slowly rubbed it back and forth over the cowboy's lubed-up hole. Nudging just the head of his cock in, Calvin stopped and waited for the cowboy to take the lead. They were still for a moment, then gradually the cowboy began to back up onto Calvin's cock. Calvin held him by the hips and met his speed, thrusting slowly and deeply. Maria fingered herself at the same speed as the men's thrusting, wanting desperately to fuck herself with something hard. Not prepared to leave the moment, she looked around her for anything suitable for penetration. There on the windowsill lay the big screwdriver she'd used to reassemble the bed and the dining table. Grabbing it by the metal part, she kicked off her shorts and knickers and began to tease at her slippery hole with the smooth ribbed handle as she watched the cowboy being fucked, Calvin's sheathed cock sliding in and out of him at a steady pace. Finally, Maria slipped the handle end into her throbbing pussy and began to fuck herself rhythmically, her knees in the air and her feet curled around the armrests of the chair.

To Maria's delight, the fucking seemed to go on and on at a steady rhythm. She could see that both men were aching to come but were holding it back for as long as they could. Both of their faces expressed in turn the beautiful and the animal elements of sexual pleasure. She continued to match her own thrusts with theirs, pausing when she felt like she was about to tip over the edge. Suddenly the men began to pick up speed. Maria followed suit. Calvin began to slam his cock into the cowboy's arse. The muscles in his own arse were coved with tension and his whole body glistened with sweat. As the cowboy pushed back to meet him, Maria fucked herself hard with the ridged handle and vigorously rubbed her clit. Then, wanting a little of what the cowboy was getting, she discarded the screwdriver and used her now free hand to tease at her arsehole. She sighed deeply as she inserted a wet finger just inside her arse and began to stroke her sphincter while shallowly thrusting. She was pushed beyond the edge as she watched the cowboy's orgasm—his face contorted in ecstasy, come shooting out of his cock and landing on the other side of the bed. In turn, Calvin shot his hot load as he was milked by the muscle spasms going on in the cowboy's tight hole. Maria's arsehole began to clench around her finger and she responded by rubbing her clit faster and harder. As she came, her whole body shuddered and a grunt forced its way out of her mouth. She felt a surge in her pussy and gasped as a stream of ejaculate shot from her spasming cunt. She felt the release through her whole body. Her orgasm began to slow, and Maria watched as Calvin finally collapsed, leaning on the cowboy's back. It was as though the three of them had let out a collective sigh. The men slumped down together on the pristine bed and Calvin brought his arm around the cowboy's waist and pulled him close.

I think I'm going to like living here, thought Maria, as she sank back in her chair and lit a cigarette.

MATTHEW, MARK, LUKE AND JOHN

Alison Tyler

I didn't mean to fuck all of them.
Matthew, Mark, Luke and John
Guard the bed that I lie on...

I'm generally not that kind of a girl.
Four corners to my bed
Four angels round my head...

If anything, I'm fiercely monogamous...or
always have been in the past.
One to watch and one to pray
And two to bear my soul away.

But I'd never tutored four guys before. Never
found myself attracted to four different men at
the same time. In my defense, it simply couldn't
be helped. They were each so unique, and so

willing. And once I'd taken one into my bed, I found turning the next one down too difficult to fathom.

Of course, other people saw the whole situation in a different light:

"Why in the hell are you taking that class?" my mother had asked sternly, when I'd read off my schedule.

"French? I've always wanted to learn French."

"Not French," she huffed. "The other one."

"Ancient Greek Art?" I tried next, grimacing at the audible sound of her anger steaming through the phone receiver. "You know I was hoping to go to Athens next summer..."

"The religious one," she interrupted. "The Jesus one."

I'd signed up for the 8:00 a.m. Christian Iconography class because it suited my schedule, not my spirituality. I was done by 9:30, able to make 10:00 a.m. French three days a week, and then finished until my late afternoon art history lecture, which gave me time for my job at a weekly newspaper.

The iconography class was my last choice, but the only one still open by the time my lottery number for class sign-ups was called. I kept reminding myself that it was important to take the appropriate amount of credits each semester. I even pretended that Christian Iconography was bound to be useful in my future life. Although how useful in my future love life, I couldn't really appreciate.

Three days a week, I found myself walking down the steep hill from dorm to quad, trying desperately to memorize the various icons we'd been discussing. For a nonpracticing Jewish girl, the subject might as well have been in Greek. (Except I was doing fine in Ancient Greek Artifacts.)

"Do you like it?" my mom asked after the first week.

"Sure," I told her. "What's not to like?"

Matthew, Mark, Luke and John
Guard the bed that I lie on.

I singsonged the nursery rhyme as I headed into class.

Four corners to my bed
Four angels round my head...

And I took my standard spot at the back of the lecture hall, to-go coffee cup in hand, ready to learn more about art with a Christian perspective.

One to watch and one to pray
And two to bear my soul away.

The truth was, I couldn't focus fully on the slides, or the droning words of the professor. Couldn't focus properly because of my fellow classmates. Well, four to be precise. The handsome jocks in the row in front of me, who always showed up late, and who seemed to have found themselves in this lecture for the same reasons I did—nothing else was available.

I listened to them joking with each other, never saw them open a notebook, never even saw them glance up at the slide show. And I nicknamed them: Matthew, Mark, Luke and John. The dark-haired "Matthew" was the man. Redheaded "Mark" was the lion. "Luke" had shaved his head, punk-rock style, and sported more than his fair share of tattoos. He was definitely the ox. And "John," the quietest, most delicately drawn, was the eagle.

Matthew, Mark, Luke and John
Guard the bed that I lie on.

In spite of their intrusion into my fantasies, I tried my best. I took copious notes. Created flash cards. Posted assorted images on my bulletin board and over my bed. I was determined to show my disbelieving family that I could ace a class I had no interest in. Although my interest grew the week before midterms, when the foursome sent over John to ask me a question.

"Study with us?"

"Excuse me?"

"We're rancid at this. Seriously. We lost a bet and had to take the class. I have no desire to take it over again, and even less of a desire to fail without trying. You look like you know what you're doing. Will you study with us tomorrow night? Cram with us. Help us out."

"Group studying has never worked for me," I told him honestly.

"You'd rather do us one on one?"

The way he asked the question made me wonder if he might actually be suggesting something else entirely. But I pretended not to hear the innuendo, and I nodded. "Sure, that would be better." And I watched as he made out a little study schedule for the week we had left. Matthew on Monday and Thursday. Mark on Tuesday and Friday. Luke on Wednesday and Saturday.

"That only leaves Sunday for you," I said.

"I'm the smartest of the four of us," he grinned.

When the first one showed up—twenty minutes late, with a brown paper bag in hand and no backpack in sight—I started to get the feeling that maybe betting on classes wasn't the only gamble this little group took.

"I've got flash cards," I told him, ushering him into my dorm room.

"I've got vodka."

"I don't think that's going to help you pass," I smiled, trying not to sound too condescending.

"But it might help me get there—" he nodded toward my bed.

"I heard you lost a bet. That's why you're taking the class."

He nodded. He didn't look the least bit sheepish about this information.

"So you're a gambler?"

Another nod as he opened the vodka.

"Then let's place a bet of our own. You name the items on the flash cards—get at least ten correct—and I'll have a glass of that."

"I didn't bring glasses."

"A swig then," I said brightly. But Matthew had other plans. "Let's try this," he countered. "You take off your clothes and lie down on the bed. Then cover yourself all over with the flash cards. If I get one correct, I'll take the card away. Until you're totally naked."

"How's that going to help you ace the exam?"

"I'm doomed," he said. "I just want to have a little fun."

Against my better judgment, I stripped down and placed the cards strategically over my body. Matthew turned away, gentlemanlike, while I got comfortable. When I was ready, he came up on the bed at my side, gazing at the images on the cards, doing his best to try to remember what each icon represented. He failed miserably, but he was such a good sport I wound up laughing, giggling as the cards fell away, and then stopping when I saw him staring at my naked body.

Matthew, Mark, Luke and John
Guard the bed that I lie on.

The words spiraled in my head as he slid off his own clothes and met me on the mattress.

"Who would have thought Christian Iconography would be such a fucking turn-on?" he growled right before he came.

On Tuesday, I vowed to be better prepared. I had books spread out on the bed, so that there was no chance for foul play, or foreplay. And I dressed myself in a no-nonsense costume—my oldest gray sweats, my dark hair scraped back in a ponytail, my glasses in place. Mark didn't seem to notice. He showed up with his backpack, unlike Matthew. But it didn't hold books, a binder, a notebook, or even a pencil. Instead, as I watched in awe, he drew out the sexiest little lingerie set, the tags showing that he'd correctly guessed my size.

"I've got this thing for brunettes in black," he said, handing over the lacy outfit. "Especially ones who wear those cute little intellectual glasses like yours."

"Why would I put that on?" I asked him. "We're supposed to be studying."

He gave me an evil smile. "Yeah? Just like you did last night?" And embarrassment flooded through me. Mark was handsome, with his long gingery hair and easygoing smile. He located my CD player while I snipped the tags and put on the outfit, and in moments, Pink Floyd came rumbling out of the speakers.

"Don't you want to try and study?" I asked.

"You can't teach me half a semester in a night," he said softly.

"We've got two sessions," I tried valiantly. "We could get you a decent score."

He shook his head. "I've got no head for those slides," he said. "And you look good enough to eat in that thing."

Who was I to argue with a lion? He had me up on my desk in a flash, my slim legs spread as he lapped and licked me along the seam of the black satin panties.

Four corners to my bed
Four angels round my head...

I saw stars when he made me come, and then he lifted me off the desk, spun me around, and pulled down my sopping panties. He fucked me hard as I stared at the images of angels with their luminous halos, then at the study schedule John had carefully laid out for us, on the bulletin board over my desk. It would definitely take a miracle for these four boys to pass.

But it took much less than a miracle for him to make me come.

Wednesday brought Luke.

And Luke brought pot.

"I thought the pictures would look prettier if we were blasted," he said.

"Prettier, maybe," I agreed, "but I don't think you're going to learn anything."

"Oh?" he asked. "I don't think that's true at all. From what I've heard, you're an excellent tutor."

Once more, I felt myself flush, and that made Luke smile, as if he'd just won an A in a difficult class. I watched as he expertly rolled a joint and lit the tip, inhaling once before handing it over to me. When I shook my head, he gripped the nape of my neck and pulled me close, kissing me and exhaling at the same time, so that my lungs filled with the fragrant smoke.

He was right. The pictures in the books were prettier when we were stoned. We looked at all of the lambs. We looked at the ancient frescoes, the colors faded but beautiful all the same. And then we looked at each other and started to laugh.

"I'm usually high in class," he said, "that's why I never take notes."

"You don't take notes because you don't care about anything but punk rock and football."

He studied me for a moment, then grinned. "Sounds like the title to one of our songs," he said. "You're very observant."

I shrugged.

"But have you noticed me watching you?"

"Yes..."

"And wondering what you look like under your clothes."

My heart started to race. I'd promised myself that two was my limit—Matthew and Mark. That I had no room in my bed for three. But I'd lied. Luke was persistent. Sweetly stroking me through my jeans before slowly undoing the button fly. The scent of pot surrounded us. And that led quickly to the scent of sex.

Who did I think I was, forgoing studying in place of pleasure? Did I think I could keep up a schedule like this? Truthfully, I didn't think. I tried to plan educational lessons, but for six days, I wound up in bed with my pupils. One after another. I knew I'd feel responsible if these four boys failed the class. But as soon as one had left, I found myself daydreaming about the next.

Sunday should have been a day of rest. Instead, I prepared for John. I found myself wishing that he had been first. Because there was no way I was going to sleep with him. I'd worked my way through the other boys—twice each. They had to have told John what we were up to. And he had the brains of the bunch. He wouldn't give me a second glance now that he knew I'd been with his frat brothers.

Would he?

John seemed prepared to study. He liked my flash cards. He liked my color-coded notes. And he liked the way I kept glancing over the top of my glasses at him. At least, that's what he said.

"And who are these four?" he asked finally.

I must have turned the nonerotic hue of a beet. "Matthew, Mark, Luke and John," I told him, wondering if he could possibly guess that those were the names I'd given him and his buddies. Monikers I couldn't shake, even when we were fucking.

"And what are these notes about?"

"Each one is represented in a different way," I explained, trying to keep my voice steady. "The man, the lion, the ox and the eagle."

"Which one am I?" he persisted, and I realized that yes, he was the smartest of the bunch. He'd found me out.

"You can guess, can't you?"

His blue eyes lit up.

"I could guess, but I'd rather have you tell me."

"No," I said, and shook my head. "Match them up. Matthew. Mark. Luke and John. Guard the bed that I lie on. Four corners to my bed. Four angels round my head…"

There was a knock on the door then, and I felt a change take place in the boy at my side. He slid the notes away. He slowly turned off the desk light. And then he went to the door and opened it, letting in the trio, waiting there for me.

I sucked in my breath. There was no way.

No way…

But, of course, there was. The angels, coming in, lifting me up. Setting me down on the floor instead of the tiny twin bed. Taking off my clothes. Wrapping me up in their bodies and their warmth. The man. The lion. The ox. The eagle.

John, taking his time, letting the others prep me before positioning himself on top. Arms tight, pumping hard.

One to watch and one to pray
And two to bear my soul away.

Had I taught them anything?

No. They were the ones who taught me. Giving me the most extreme pleasure in that single evening. Drawing out our actions. Painting pictures with their lips on mine, their fingertips on my skin.

We didn't study at all, but we stayed up all night. Stumbling into class with bleary eyes. Laughing as the exams were passed out. Feeling as faded as one of those old frescoes, but as beautiful.

John laughed when the slides of the four apostles came up. And I knew he'd get at least one answer right. One out of many.

But you want to know all of the test results, don't you?

Well, I won't lie. They failed. Each more dismally than the next. With their study habits, they couldn't possibly pass. But that was okay.

You see, it was only a midterm.

We had plenty of time to cram before finals.

ABOUT THE AUTHORS

JACQUELINE APPLEBEE is a Black British woman who enjoys writing erotica at inopportune moments. She is a secretary by day, but has also earned a living making sex toys and silver jewelry. One of her fondest memories is of serving tea at S/M Pride, to an admiring crowd. Jacqueline has appeared in Clean Sheets, *Iridescence: Sensuous Shades of Lesbian Erotica* and *Travelrotica 2*.

KELL BRANNON lives and works in the Chicago area, and has been writing erotic material for several years. Several pieces of her work have been published in Clean Sheets. She also keeps a blog, celebrateyournaughtiness.blogspot.com, where she posts more short fiction and commentary.

BEST WOMEN'S EROTICA 2008

MORTICIA CATHERINE is a Theatre Practitioner and Performer who has been writing erotic fiction for women for some time—although she only just decided to submit her work after starting her MA in Contemporary Theatre Practice. She enjoys reading erotic fiction and is currently looking at ways of combining erotic imagery and fiction into Contemporary Performance. She is not "afraid of porn"—but prefers her explicit sex to have an edge. She likes tattoos, piercings, burlesque, costume and beautiful shoes, though not always in that order.

LOLA DAVID is a blogger, dabbler in erotica writing, and professional aficionado of all fabulous writers. She's a twenty-nine-year-old wife and mother of two toddlers who lives in the SF Bay Area.

ELLAREGINA is an artist and writer living near—but not inside—New York City's Washington Square Arch. She enjoys penning bedtime stories for grown-ups. Awards include a New York Foundation for the Arts Fellowship and residencies at Yaddo and The MacDowell Colony, among others. This is her first published story, and you can find her at myspace.com/ellaregina.

A. D. R. FORTE's erotic short stories appear in *Lips Like Sugar* and *Lust* from Cleis Press. Her work is also featured in several of Black Lace's *Wicked Words* collections.

SCARLETT FRENCH is a short-story writer and a poet. She lives in London's East End with her partner and a pugnacious marmalade cat. Her erotic fiction has appeared in *Best Lesbian Erotica 2005, Va Va Voom, First Timers: True Stories of*

Lesbian Awakening, Tales of Travelrotica for Lesbians and *Best Women's Erotica 2007*. She is currently working on her first novel but is repeatedly distracted by the urge to write filth.

R. GAY is a writer and graduate student whose work appears in many anthologies including *Best American Erotica 2004*, several editions of *Best Lesbian Erotica* and *The Mammoth Book of Best New Erotica*, among others.

Decadent, devilish and delightful are three words that have been used to describe the work of K. L. GILLESPIE. She wrote her first story, aged seven, about a child-eating nun and since then she has worked as a music journalist, art gallery curator and screenwriter. She is a regular contributor to *TANK* magazine and has recently been published in *Wicked: Sexy Tales of Legendary Lovers, Best Women's Erotica 2006, 'Dying for It: Stories of Sex and Death* and *The Mammoth Book of Erotica*. Her eagerly anticipated first novel, *Jesus Loves Penge,* is out later this year.

KAY JAYBEE lives in Devon, England. She's had a number of stories published by Cleis Press (*Lips Like Sugar; Best Women's Erotica 2007; Lust*) amd Black Lace (*Sex and Music*). She is currently awaiting the publication of a story in *The Mammoth Book of Lesbian Erotica* (Mammoth Books). Kay has also had a variety of poems and stories featured on the web site OystersandCholocate.com. Her story, "Tied to the Kitchen Sink" is now a podcast read by Violet Blue on her Open Source Sex web site.

JESSICA LENNOX has lived in several states, from coast to coast, and is currently residing in New Jersey, while working in Manhattan. She has always had a love for erotic fiction and hopes to someday be recognized as an accomplished writer. Her hobbies and interests include gender theory, motorcycles, travel, sports and of course, books!

MSPRISM is Irish but works and lives between Ireland, the United Kingdom and Greece. Sailing and writing are her two main interests. She has had several articles published in a variety of arts magazines and was once a syndicated cartoonist for an Irish newspaper group to pay her way through college.

CERISE NOIRE has enjoyed telling stories ever since she learned how to form sentences, and she's been fascinated by all things sexual for as long as she's been aware of sex. Her writing can be found on Literotica.com, Vibrator.com, InkyBlueAllusions, and Good Vibrations (in the fall); this is her first foray into print. She's currently working on her first erotic novel. When not writing, or working, Cerise is reading, or supporting the red shoe industry. The number of pairs she owns is unreasonable—especially since she prefers to walk barefoot.

PEONY currently lives in a little corner of Melbourne, Australia. When not writing erotic fiction or blogging until very late at night, she can be found at the rollerama, the tattoo shop or drinking red wine and listening to Tom Waits. She loses chess games against her partner often and with little grace and is forced to take solace in long baths, sweet food or (more) wine. She dreams of a laptop in a tree house in the tropics, a cute puppy and more time with her man, as well as the ability to skate backward with finesse. She also believes that words written and spoken have the power to move, entice and delight us long after images have faded from view.

MIEL ROSE is a low-income, rural, chubby, scrappy, queer high femme of Italian/Danish and Irish/Scottish decent. She is a total plant lover, in every sense of the word. Her first accepted porno story will be published in *Tough Girls 2: Down and Dirty Dyke Erotica*.

DONNA GEORGE STOREY's previous erotica publications include *She's on Top: Stories of Female Dominance and Male Submission, He's on Top: Stories of Male Dominance and Female Submission, Garden of the Perverse: Fairy Tales for Twisted Adults, Taboo: Forbidden Fantasies for Couples, Love at First Sting, Best American Erotica 2006, Mammoth Book of Best New Erotica 4, 5* and *6* and *Best Women's Erotica 2005, 2006* and *2007*. Her novel set in Japan, *Amorous Woman*, will be released in the United Kingdom as part of Orion's Neon erotica series.

Called a "trollop with a laptop" by the *East Bay Express* and a "literary siren" by *Good Vibrations*, ALISON TYLER is naughty and she knows it. Her sultry short stories have appeared in more than seventy anthologies including *Sweet Life* (Cleis), *Sex at the Office* (Virgin), and *Glamour Girls* (Alyson). She is the author of more than twenty-five erotic novels, and the editor of more than thirty-five explicit anthologies, including *A Is for Amour, B Is for Bondage, C Is for Coeds* and *D Is for Dress-Up* (all just out from Cleis). Please visit alisontyler.com for more information or myspace.com/alisontyler if you'd like to be her friend.

AMY WADHAMS was born and raised in southeast Texas, and married too young. Now she's attempting to start a career doing what she does best...thinking dirty.

SASKIA WALKER's erotic fiction appears in over forty anthologies, including *Caught Looking, She's on Top, A Is for Amour, Secrets Volume 19, Naughty Spanking Stories 2, The Mammoth Book of Best New Erotica Volume 5,* and *Kink.* She is the author of several novellas as well as the erotic novels *Along for the Ride, Double Dare* and *Reckless.* Please visit www.saskiawalker.co.uk for more information.

XAN WEST is the pseudonym of an NYC BDSM educator. Xan's erotica can be found in *Best SM Erotica 2* and the forthcoming *Got A Minute?, Love at First Sting, Men on the Edge,* and *Hide and Seek.* Xan can be reached at xan_west@yahoo.com.

JORDANA WINTERS is a twentysomething Canadian writer of women's erotica. Her online credits include Steamy Audio, A Woman's Goodnight, Forbidden Publications, The Erotic Woman, Ruthie's Club, Oysters & Chocolate, Extasybooks, and Thermoerotic. Jordana's print credits include *Best Women's Erotica 2008, 2007 & 2006, Sex & Seduction, Uniform Sex* and *Erotic Tales.* When not hiding behind her computer telling filthy tales, Jordana is an often-disenchanted administrative whore. Jordana's interests include working out, chillin' out, tattoos, doing as much and as little as possible and pissing people off. Jordana admits to spending too much time living stories built in her own head. Visit her at jordanawinters.tripod.com.

ABOUT THE EDITOR

VIOLET BLUE is the best-selling, award-win-
ning author and editor of numerous books on
sex and sexuality, all currently in print, a number of which have been translated into several
languages; she has also contributed to a number of nonfiction sex anthologies. Violet is the
sex columnist for the *San Francisco Chronicle* with a weekly column titled "Open Source
Sex," and has a podcast of the same name that
frequents iTunes' top ten. She is a San Francisco sex educator who lectures at University of
California branches and community teaching
institutions, and writes about erotica, pornog-
raphy, sexual pleasure and health for major
publications and blogs. Violet is a professional
sex blogger and femmebot; an author at Me-
troblogging San Francisco (Metblogs); a video

correspondent for Geek Entertainment Television; she is on the Gawker Media payroll as girl friday contributor and editor at Fleshbot. In January 2007, Violet was named a *Forbes* Web Celeb 25. She is a San Francisco native and human blog. Violet has been featured by numerous publications including *Wired,* the *Wall Street Journal* and *Newsweek,* and has written for media outlets such as *O, The Oprah Magazine* and *Forbes.* Her website tinynibbles.com is home to her popular sex blog, and her nerdy culture blog is techyum.com.